Vacuum Stories

By Harry McNabb

DFWD, TX

Free Tongue Press
Dallas, TX

Preferred method of contact is carrier pigeon
But if absent of pigeons, FB or Insta will do

First Edition

ISBN: 978-0-578-51893-0

Design, Layout, Edits: Tom Farris
Front Cover: Rachel Eastman

Noitcudortni

These stories were written in a social vacuum i.e. when you read them you're not going to be spoken to, you're going to observe me speaking amongst myself. None of these stories saw a workshop. No one told me to write them. I wrote them because I didn't know what else to do. On the next page there is a list of story-titles with page numbers. Start with the title that interests you the most.

Hector Mendoza

One day, God ate his own face. Then he had no face. With his non-face, God ate the faces of every self-aware creature in the universe.

So then, at this juncture, this junk-ship we call linear time and three-dimensional space, no one has a face.

Most of the time, everyone sits around and cries.

Once a month, we have a pep-rally.

During the pep-rally, we are allowed to wear casual clothes. We cheer from the bleachers as god sneezes golden stags from his nose. The golden stags gallop around our non-faces. Then, we have a sack race. Then, mostly, we go back to sitting around and crying by ourselves.

This goes for everyone. Everyone, that is, except Hector Mendoza. This is because Hector Mendoza has the power to eat non-faces. Man, Hector Mendoza can eat your non-face so that you don't have a face or a non-face or anything.

Man, Hector Mendoza can make you practically dead.

He even made God practically dead.

He made both one silverfish and two okapi practically dead, man.

He made a golden stag dead when it

ran through his section at the frikking pep rally, man.

Every time Hector Mendoza eats a non-face, more of the face god ate comes back.

Right now, people are just learning about Hector Mendoza. On this past Thursday, like, THE ONLY THURSDAY practically EVER in linear time and three-dimensional space, Hector Mendoza got interviewed on the San Antonio local news. The news anchor said "BOY-EEE!" when Hector Mendoza ate the non-face off of an old man who had not had a face his whole entire life.

Afterwards the old man said to a reporter "you've gotta do some work and be good to people, because we don't realize this but we don't have anything and we aren't anything, so we gotta take decisive action and move around the places we can move around in and do some stuff." He seemed energetic and motivated.

No one knows much about Hector Mendoza. His Wikipedia page says that he is a high school student and doesn't have any parents. His Wikipedia page also says that he is 15 years old and is Hispanic-American and is a U.S. citizen. Another thing his Wikipedia page said is he appeared on a KENS 5 TV station and that the news anchor said "boy," very loud. Furthermore, his Wikipedia page says that despite his Hispanic heritage, Hector Mendoza cannot speak Spanish.

Yesterday, on Monday, Hector Mendoza appeared on channel 5 again and he ate the non-face of a dog and one of god's angels and the anchor. The anchor said that he's not working for channel 5 anymore. Hector Mendoza said he didn't want the anchor to stop working, that it wasn't his intention. Hector

Mendoza gave the news anchor a hug. Apart from those events, the angel dissolved into some crystals which flew all around San Antonio curing people of cancer. The dog left the newsroom and bit a depressed intern. I was really excited. I brought my pot of macaroni which I eat with hot sauce and oregano into my mom's room to watch Hector Mendoza's appearance and we were both happy as we watched.

On Yahoo News this morning, there was tell of the appearance and the non-face eating, as well as, at the bottom of the article, mention of the news that Hector Mendoza will be appearing on Anderson Cooper on CNN. I'm excited about watching it with my non-face.

When I was an unrealized future occurrence and god ate my face it felt like somebody hungry and ferocious took something away from me that I needed to use and was using slowly.

"Like the white teeth of pain," is the way I am choosing to describe it in my journal. I'm only now talking about it in my journal because of Hector Mendoza.

Hector Mendoza, on last Thursday, the only Thursday, the first day EVER of reality as far as I can see or am concerned, talked about how everyone sits around and cries. Like I knew that I sit around and cry, and that my mom sits around and cries, and that this girl I used to date and her parents all sat around and cried, but I wasn't sure about everyone else, y'know, and because I know now I feel happier. I don't know if that's a good thing, but it feels like it is.

2 Mollusks

2 mollusks went to work. When they passed eachother at work, they felt awkward. She, because she saw him look away from her and he because he didn't want to suffer the embarrassment of another awkward exchange. But even without getting to the "exchange" stage, their being near one another, seeing one another, was awkward.

2 months earlier, the male mollusk had sent the female mollusk 23 text messages. When the male mollusk tried to make a humorous comment about vaginal fluid and told the female mollusk 2 text messages later that this

was his way of flirting, the female mollusk got all irate and told him she wasn't attracted to him anymore.

She had lied. She was a dirty, lying mollusk!

The male mollusk apologized the next morning.

The female mollusk said it was okay, even though it wasn't. It was awkward.

The male mollusk watched the female mollusk's ass when she cleaned tables with her radula. She had a big ass for a white-girl mollusk. Her ass made him want to say "damn" in a ghetto way.

One day, the mollusks went out with a group to a Korean Spa that owned a personality-swapping machine. The 2 mollusks put their heads in the machine and got new personalities. The two new personalities didn't mind having sex with each other. So they had sex.

The new personalities decided it would be cool to set a timer for the personalities to change back to the mollusk's original personalities in the middle of sex. This was arranged.

The switch happened, but the two kept on kissing and fucking because kissing and fucking feels nice. Neither of them were egregiously physically unattractive. And then they had an honest post-coital conversation. And the awkwardness left their bodies like fungus detaching from a once moist, now hot and dry rock.

And it was good that they'd had sex then, because if they hadn't, they'd have had to carry all that awkwardness with them to Hogwarts for their 5th year. They were the first Mollusk-wizards in Hogwarts history.

They had to look sharp and represent their families well. The mollusk community was counting on them. "United we stand divided we fall" thought the male mollusk, a week before they were scheduled to board the Hogwarts express. Then he thought "united in sex we stand, divided in awkwardness we fall."

The female mollusk had no such thoughts. Her thoughts were "git r done" and then 567 minutes of lawnmower noise.

When they talked to God in their respective daily prayers of thanksgiving, God said "no, thank YOU."

The Male mollusk lived to be 71 years old. The female mollusk lived to be 90 years old. They were both funny-ass mollusks when they entered their twilight years. They were the variety of geriatric mollusk who wandered around naked and said dumb shit.

The white teenage mollusks in their neighborhood were able to use the male and female mollusks in their memoirs. The male and female mollusks were wizards and artistic inspiration.

When they both died and went to mollusk heaven, they met each other again, with the appearances of their young selves.

The male mollusk hit on the female mollusk by asking her out for heaven-drinks. She declined because she had a prior engagement with her mollusk friend who was also in heaven.

The male mollusk texted her from a bar. He asked her if she'd ever eaten pussy. She said no. He asked her if she'd sucked a guys dick. She said yes. He asked if semen tastes different person to person, and that he was wondering because he felt vaginal fluid tasted different from female to female.

2 texts later he said that the text messages he'd sent were his attempts at flirting.

And the female mollusk presented the male mollusk with her cold, mollusk shoulder.

When the male mollusk wasn't drunk anymore, he said "sorry about last night"
and the female mollusk responded "don't worry about it."

They didn't work together anymore, because there was no work in heaven. They didn't work together so they didn't see eachother and what contact they had quickly eroded. They went their separate ways and decided to see what heaven had to offer.

And you know what the best thing heaven has to offer is?

You can eat as much food as you want and never get fat.

Crane-Base Hunting, Ungowa

It was raining. The rain was ghastly.
Here came Harry, dressed like a
knight, but in modern times. A knight
in modern times wears a blazer and
sunglasses and doesn't look stupid.
He went down the street looking for a
crane. He'd seen the top of a crane
from the library downtown, and on this
day he thought he'd never seen the
base of a crane before so he went
crane-base hunting. Down Akard
Street. It was raining, but his blazer
emitted a type of radiation that turned
the rain to steam. He had about 40
dollars in his wallet because he had
gone to an ATM. At this juncture he
congratulated himself on having the

initiative to go to an ATM, *yeah*! Now he could buy some good train passes. Downtown Dallas is a poor man's New York City. Part of it looks like it's in the 80s and part of it looks like an exotic palace. *Hurray for that*, said Harry, pulling out a Virginia Slim and lighting it with a match. He put the match out like an African-American woman wagging her finger and saying "oh no you didn't!" He puffed that Virginia slim, ungowa. There were homeless people walking past him. A great guy he knew from otherwheres was handing out the Street Zine, a newspaper that published content by the Homeless of Dallas. He used one of his 20 dollar bills on some Street Zine.

"God bless you, man. God bless you!"

Harry gave him a hug. A long hug. And then he went on. *To the crane*, he thought. To the crane.

Though it was 20 times the suggested donation for a copy of Street Zine, Harry thought 20 dollars was a good amount of money to give a Street Zine employee. If a Street Zine employee made 10 dollars they met their quota and kept their job. If they made 10 dollars and then another 10 dollars – that was 10 bonus points that went towards them getting their own area. Though, Harry thought, John, the guy he had patroned did already have his own area. Harry guessed that the money would go towards John maybe getting a second chance if he didn't meet his quota on a different day.
He walked past his friend Jaime's apartment. Jaime had a bigscreen TV in his apartment. The elevator made a submarine noise when it went up. Harry played music with Jaime. He looked in the garage of the apartment building and saw a white patch next to Jaime's car. The white patch had been caused by Harry's vomit.

Harry saw Jaime on the street corner. Harry hadn't been planning to run into Jaime. Jaime was also dressed like a knight, but like a knight going for some R and R. His sleeves were rolled up. Jaime also had a tie because he worked in a law firm, Harry remembered. Harry did not work in a law firm. Harry owned and managed a movie theatre called The Golden Harratorium. The Harratorium's bathrooms had gold-leaf toilet paper. It was the Ritz, that theatre with its goldleaf toilet paper.

It was Harry's first edict as manager to make all of the popcorn salt Cajun flavored, so that people could get some Cajun popcorn, which was better. Harry would walk around the lobby of the theatre drinking a strawberry malt. His hair would be combed very nicely, like God's hair, when he did this ungowa.
Harry hailed Jaime.

"Hello Jaime. It's raining and I am talking to you. What's going on?"

"Hello Harry. I'm going on my walk that I go on."

"Oh"

"and then after my walk, Harry, I am going to go out with my girlfriend Stephanie and we are going to eat steak and then we are going to go home and touch each others's business."

Jaime pronounced others' "otherses."

"Oh okay"

Silence between the two knights.

Then Jaime said: "Harry, would you like to go get a blonde roast with me at Starfox?"
Starfox was a coffee restaurant.

Besides coffee, they had mean hamburgers.

Harry said "sure."

"So what are you doing around here anyway" said Jaime as they turned left on a street called Narwhale Bukakke.

"I was looking for the base of a crane"

"Yeah?" said the J man

"Yeah." said the H-man

"That's a quirky thing to be doing with your do's - I mean, your time."

Jaime had been trying not to say silly things. He had been trying to be more direct lately. Because he said "do's" instead of time he moved the bracelet casually from his left wrist to his right. Harry did not notice this. Jaime had intended for Harry not to notice this. Jaime's girlfriend, Stephanie, had made him a quirky bracelet. A black piece of string with beads that spelled out Jaime's name. If Jaime wanted, he could untie it easily and rearrange the letters and make other words out of the letters J A I M and E.

"Yeah," said Harry, "I'm just interested, you know. Never seen it before, thought I'd try and find it. See where it is, what it looks like."

Jaime took Harry through a little entrail that went underneath an office building. Harry thought entrail was the correct word for this sort of clandestine passage. They went past an older woman and as they went past Harry turned his head and looked at her bottom. He had a thing for older women. But he was on a quest, so he couldn't engage her. She looked happy and was fat. She probably weighed like what like 170 ungowa. Harry rubbed his hands together like Kramer from Seinfeld.

"My uncle Matty said that this entrail runs all the way across the whole of Dallas," the J Man said.

Harry did not respond. He nodded politely, but really, he didn't give a rat's butthole if the entrail ran all the way across Dallas. He would have social coffee with the J Man. But then he had to find this Crane Base. But they were further delayed because the J Man had to go to the bathroom.

"Just wait here," said Jaime

"Yes, dad," said Harry

Jaime laughed a little too hard and pointed at Harry and then pointed at his own head, laughing awkwardly as he walked to the restroom. Once inside the restroom, Jaime put the bracelet on his left wrist. Jaime sat on the toilet and pooped in the toilet. He also peed a little. When he had finished pooping and peeing, he wiped his penis and his butthole with toilet paper. This took him 7 minutes. Meanwhile Harry stood around in the entrail thinking about that old fat woman. Her affirmation would debloat his ego and make him a nicer person, he thought. She would evacuate all the semen that he couldn't evacuate through mere masturbation. All the white mass huddled near his prostate, he imagined.

The entrail was wide. You could drive a car down the path they'd been walking. The floor was marbled and there were little windows near the ceiling. It was a very peaceful entrail, Harry thought. Good Feng Shui for an entrail.

Harry was bored bored bored bored. But then he saw a speck of dust on the floor and he just thought like wow what an awesome speck of dust ungowa ungowa o my god. And Harry started digging on that speck of dust.

Looking at it really close on the floor. Getting on his knees and moving his head right up to it. Harry's entire world was all about this speck of dust. He was going to write a *À La Recherche Du Temps Perdu* about that speck of dust, but then Jaime came out of the bathroom and he forgot about it.

They walked for miles on the marble. *When are we going to stop*, thought Harry. But then they did stop and Jaime found that his uncle had been wrong. Jaime kicked a dog, he was so mad. Harry intervened and put the dog back on its dog-stand. Then Jaime started laughing. His anger had been fake anger. He had been trying to make a joke. Harry didn't find the joke funny. Jaime scratched the back of his head.

They went outside. The rain was still ghastly.

"The rain is still bad" said Harry

Jaime drank a raindrop and then spit it out. The dirt molecule in the drop burrowed into one of his teeth.

"Do you like the writer William S. Burroughs?" said Jaime

Harry didn't hear Jaime.

"Weren't we going to go to the Starfox and get burgers and coffee?" asked Harry.

"Oh yeah," said Jaime.

So they winked their left eyes seven times, their right eyes nine times, and their left eyes seven times again, and teleported to Starfox.

This was a special Starfox in an office building. There were steps you went down to get to glass doors, as well as a pineapple tree, and a palm tree, and a waterfall. A pool formed at the base of the waterfall and in the pool there were giant orange and blue eels. "We'll have to feed the eels some hamburgers later," said Jaime. There was a little girl alien with her three alien papas and one fat alien mama feeding little pieces of hamburger to the eels. One eel's head rested above the water poised to catch burger-fragments.

"Have you had a mocha burger yet," asked Jaime

"No," said Harry. "I think I'm just going to stick with a plain old fashioned nacho burger."

"But we've gotta get some blonde roast, right?" said Jaime

"Yep," said Harry with a wee smile as he folded his glasses and put them in his front pocket. "Gotta have me a blonde roast." Harry wore a t-shirt under his blazer that had the word

AFFLICTION emblazoned upon it in capital letters. He liked it because it let people know that he already knew something was wrong with him, so they didn't have to say anything about it because he was okay with himself and stuff.

"Do you like the Clash?" asked Jaime.

"Yeah," said Harry, "they're alright. I like Sandinista the most because it has that rap song on it and 'Police On My Back.' I love me some 'Police On My Back.'

"I had sex with a police officer once," said Jaime.

"Was it fun?" asked Harry

"Yeah, she wore her whole uniform except for her pants."

"Damn."

"Damn yes!" said Jaime. He paused for a moment and then casually took the bracelet off his left hand and put it on his right. Then he imagined an image of a squirrel eating grass with a narrator talking about the squirrel eating the grass.

The three people in line in front of them were clones of Harry's creative writing teacher, Deva Arumagam from way back when when he was in a creative writing class. All of the clones's hair still had highlights like he remembered, though in the case of one clone there were strands of gray interspersed. The gray and gold and black came together in a cool way and looked really cool.

"Hey Deva!" he said to one of the clones.

The clone turned around with a look on her face that said "Do I know you?" and that's when Harry realized that neither she nor any of the other clones were the real McCoy.

Nevertheless, he asked, "how're you doing, Deva?"

"My name isn't Deva," said the clone without Real McCoy Deva's trademark indian accent. "My name is Xena Wondershowzen."

"Okay," said Harry. "Sorry."

"Do you like Star Trek?" asked Jaime.

"Yes," said Harry, "It is my favoritest show of all the shows."

"Yesterday, my stepmother told me that her dermatologist is named Doctor McCoy like the Doctor on Star Trek."

"That's so funny," said Harry. "I also had a stepmother with a dermatologist named Doctor McCoy."

"Wow!" said Jaime. "Like, wouldn't it be funny if we had like the same life?"

Harry didn't say anything.

Jaime put the bracelet on his other wrist.

It was their turn to conduct transactions. And once they had coffee, Harry thought, then he could go find the base of the crane. Harry ordered some stuff. J man ordered some stuff. They sat down at a little table and both of them crossed their legs while they sat. It is wrong to cross my legs but it feels comfortable, both Jaime and Harry thought. Xena Wondershowzen and the other Deva clones sat chattering in the corner of the Starfox. They looked like an Indian version of Sex and the City.

"Draw something!" Said Harry suddenly.

"Okay!" said Jaime, eager to go along with Harry's impulsiveness. "What should I draw on?"

"Here," said Harry.

"Will pencil show up on it?"

"Only one way to find out,"

So Jaime drew the star trek symbol on the large piece of plexiglass Harry had given him. While he was drawing, an alien from outside came and sucked on the glass. The alien child sucked all the graphite off the plexiglass. Jaime did not expect this to happen and became irritated.

"I am an irritated porpoise," said Jaime, using an expression that was popular on TV.

"You will enjoy the water later, Jaime," said Harry. "You can keep the piece of plexiglass and draw on it later."

"But the first drawing I made was so much better!" Jaime's irritated talking was loud enough to make the trio of Deva Arumagam clones throw irritated looks at Harry and Jaime. Their irritated looks irritated Harry.

Just then, a giant Salamander flew past the window. It was fifty feet long. The rush of wind it left in its wake ruffled the palm trees. Big Kahuna, thought Harry. Harry of course didn't say "Big Kahuna," because it would be impolite to interrupt Jaime while he was complaining.

The offending alien had gone to the bathroom to try sucking up all the toilet water. The alien had a large stem protruding from its head, which was presently resting in the water like a fishing line. There were bubble noises coming from the alien's head. The alien thought about how she was similar to Earth-bees. She did the same thing earth-bees did except her flowers were toilets and she was a female. Earth bee females were lucky, she thought. They just sat on their bottoms getting laid. The alien thought about getting laid. She thought about getting fucked by a proboscis monkey's nose.

Harry finished his stuff and decided he wanted to continue his search for the Crane's base.

"Gooooooooooodbyeeeeeeee Jayyyyyymmeeeeeeeeeee," said Harry in slow motion.

"Seeeeeeeeeeeeeeyaaaaaaaaaaaaaaaa, taaaaaaaaaakkkkkkkeeee iiiiiiiiiiitttt eeeeeaaaasssssssyyyyyyyyy," said Jaime in slow motion.

Walking through the Starfox's courtyard, and up the steps, Harry couldn't figure out where the entrail had taken him in relation to where he had been when he saw the crane. He wanted some crane-base, ungowa.

"Ay, where the Crane-base at?" Harry asked a little girl who was walking the opposite way down the sidewalk.

"Which crane-base?" asked the little girl, stopping. She held a tiny hotwheels car in her hand.

"The base of big red-and-white," said Harry

"You mean Big red-and-white, the Johnny Unitas of cranes if all the cranes in the world were the NFL?" said the little girl.

"Yeah, maybe," said Harry.

"Big Red-and-White lives in Kuala Lumpur," said the little girl.

"Well, uh, sorry, I was trying to be poetic," said Harry.

"I don't care," said the little girl.

"Thanks," said Harry, smiling nervously.

"No," said the little girl. "I don't mean 'I don't care,' in a nice way. Please specify the crane type a little more? This is a local crane?"

"Yes," said Harry, wiping the smile off of his face. "It's red and white and has little blue flags on top, ungowa."

"Why did you say ungowa," asked the little girl.

"Because I was excited," said Harry.

"Well, you shouldn't have said it," said the little girl. "It was unnecessary. You may very well want to show me you're excited, but why you want to show me, I don't know. Your being excited has nothing to do with me. Maybe if your emotions are making you excited and you cannot help it, that is okay, but your saying 'ungowa' gives the impression that you are trying to draw attention to yourself and that makes me not like you. If you wanted my attention, I would prefer that you were polite and asked me for attention, rather than going about it in a circuitous, passive way."

"I'm sorry, I don't think about it that much," said Harry

"So you're stupid?" said the little girl

"Yes," said Harry.

"Okay," said the little girl, "I can accept that. My name is Michelle. Would you like to share bunny flesh to make peace?"

"Sounds good," said Harry.

So, Harry and Michelle ate a bunny together. Michelle stung the bunny's brain dead with a club. They ate the bunny at the Starfox Harry had just left. Jaime was still sitting in the Starfox, staring out the window at the palm trees. Harry and the little girl sat outside, eating bunny flesh behind a family of obese aliens from Planet McDonalds. Harry saved some of the bunny flesh in his pocket to feed to the eels when they left, but he forgot about feeding the eels because it stopped raining.

"Dang," said the little girl. "Why'd the rain stop? I was enjoying it. It was like a gentle, warm wet thing tickling me."

"I'm glad it stopped," said Harry. "It will be easier to find my crane-base, now that the rain-haze has dissipated."

"Awwww!" said the little girl. "I was hoping you'd want to stay and eat a squirrel with me. Do you really have to go look for that crane?"

"Yep," said Harry. "It's important to stick with your plans. It makes you healthier. Even though sticking to your plans is hard and may sometimes seem silly, you have to. Plans are like the crane-base a crane-neck rests on."

"Oh, okay," said the little girl. "But we should have sex tonight."

"Wha?" said Harry, "but you're a little girl! I don't want to have sex with you!"

"No," said the little girl, "I'm an accelerated-aging clone. I hatched this morning. By tonight, I'll be 18."

"Eh, maybe tomorrow morning," said Harry. "We can have sex when you're 40."

"Deal!" said the little girl,"You're a fun stupid-person to talk to!"

"And you're a fun, smart little girl," said Harry.

So Harry left. He walked 20 paces when he remembered he had forgotten to ask Michelle where the crane was. He turned around.

But she had already teleported.

He had her phone number written on a piece of bunny flesh, but he decided he could probably find the crane-base by his own intuition.

He also decided that he should buy the afternoon edition of Street Zine. So he bought it. He didn't like this Street Zine vendor too much so he only gave him 10 dollars. 10 dollars was enough for the Street Zine vendor, Michael Silverback-Gorilla, to meet his quota. This was the article on the front page of the afternoon edition of Street Zine:

"Spiderman Cloned:
sometimes-
negatively,
sometimes
positively thought
about webslinger to
carry 100 new
friends in papoose
on back
On a day rained
with rain, more
than the natural
phenomenon of
precipitation
participated in the
engenderment of
new, little things. A
UT Southwestern
Medical Center
spokesperson
announced that the
institution has
successfully cloned
Peter Parker, A.K.A.
the superhero,
Spiderman a record

100 times. It is the most Spiderman, or any superhero for that matter has been cloned.

"I wanted to make my cloning special," said Peter Parker. "Originally, I wanted there to be one Spiderman for every city in the world. I started creating uniforms too. But during the whole process, I noticed I didn't really like making uniforms and really liked giving trigger-happy scientists my DNA, so I don't really have any purpose for these new, special people, as of yet."

As with any clone, post-individuation will be a psychological challenge for the Spider-clones. Neo-Superman's depression and over-eating were documented voluminously by street zine. "People would come up to me and say, 'Superman save us from this Volcanic eruption,' and I'd say 'Superman? I'm not Superman.' And fly off all emo-like. I was so immature and selfish back then." But Neo-Superman coped with his clonality by wearing a different costume from Superman's and growing a beard. He looks nothing like Superman now. He lives in Mozambique as his alter-ego, Michael Butt.

The spider-babies were crawling all over the walls in Peter Parker's house. Because Mary Jane Parker only has two breasts, the couple has purchased a swimming pool-sized milk-reservoir appended by100 hoses.

The new parents were running around trying to stop the little tykes from trampling one another to death, so your correspondent was not able to ween many words from them. Spiderman plans to make a book out of the designs for the costumes he will not be forcing his clones to wear, and eventually a touring art exhibition. He says he also wants to write a book about going on the road with the touring art exhibition and another book about just being Spiderman in general, and a book of short stories following a

character based on
Spiderman but not
Spiderman himself,
a book about Neo-
Superman, and a
memoir book about
his love of
basketball."

Harry was moved by the article. It
moved him down the sidewalk without
him noticing where he was walking and
stopping and turning and navigating
to. When he read the word,
"basketball," he overheard a couple
guys talking –

"man if you turn around and look up
you get a good view of that crane."

"yeah, but we have to go look at the
smooth wall because it's smooth wall-
watching time"

Harry looked up. Eureka, he thought.
There was the crane. Now he had only

to walk to it. But how? You could
hardly get anywhere as the crow flies
in the city. There were a number of
roads you had to cross and buildings to
walk around and people and aliens to
wade through, and Harry was more
than capable of navigating them, but it
would take time and there were so
many strange and interesting things
around Harry that the crane base
would have to compete.

There were lots of women. Harry liked
women. He especially liked large
women with dark hair. And there was
one such large dark haired woman
strolling by. She had large
headphones and sunglasses and was
wearing running shorts, the way lots of
women do when they go out to do
their groceries. She had grocery bags.
She was doing her shopping.

Shopping is cool, thought Harry, I like
to shop, ungowa. My favorite things to
buy are affliction t-shirts, so people

know I have something the matter with me. Harry kept on thinking, staring at this woman's pink running short covered butt. She walked on the other side of the street, parallel to him in the same direction, the direction of the crane.

He crossed.

He came up behind her.

He drew level with her.

She looked busy.

Harry liked women who looked busy.

"Hello!" said Harry.

The woman did not hear him.

"Hello!" he said again, this time waving at her. Startled, she took off her headphones and said "what?" in a worried tone of voice.

"Nothing," said Harry, "I just wanted to say hello and talk to you."

"Oh," said the woman taken aback.

"Yes, said Harry, "What's your name," he asked.

"My name's Melinda," she said.

"Like Bill Gates's wife?" said Harry.

"Yes" – she let out a fake laugh – "just like Bill Gates's wife."

"Where do you work," asked Harry

"Long John Silvers," she said. "It's a fish restaurant."

"Oh really," said Harry. "I like fish. And lobster. And oysters."

"Well you should come by sometime," she said. "We don't have oysters or lobster, but we have fish."
"Cool," said Harry. "I totally should."

"So what do you do?" she asked.

"I own and operate a movie theatre," said Harry.

"Wow!" she said. "That's so cool! I love movies!"

"What kind of movies do you like?" asked Harry.

"Well, I don't like any particular kind of movies," she said. "I just really like being in movie theatres, like with all those people in a dark room completely quiet and focused on the screen...I guess, like you know how there are social drinkers? I'm a social moviegoer."

"Huh," said Harry. "I can dig that."

"Which movie theatre do you own?"
she asked.

"The Harratorium," said Harry. "I
named it after myself."

"Wow!" she said. "You're Harry
McNabb? The mysterious yet flawed
owner of the Harratorium?"

"The very same," said Harry.

"Why, I've been going to your theatre
since it opened. I haven't been there
in the last 5 years since I've been
away at college, but almost every
Saturday I'd go there with my friends
or by myself and sit in your movie
theatre, not paying attention to what
was going on in the movies or
anything. Just being fascinated and
titillated by the sight of so many
complicated, egocentric human beings
transfixed by something outside of
themselves...at the mercy of it almost.

Like they were a baby being nursed by their mother, the screen."

"Ha ha!" said Harry, "I guess that's one way to look at it!"

"Yep," she said, and then stopped next to a lavish-looking building.

"This is me," she said, "It was nice chatting with you. I guess I'll see you at the theatre?"

"If you like," said Harry, "and if you like, you can also see me at a place that is not the theatre. Here's my card."

This is what the card said:

Harry McNabb
The Golden Harratorium
Founder, Owner, Manager
064876231
afflicteddude04@goldenharratorium.com

And this is what it said on the back:

"Give them pleasure. The same pleasure they have when they wake up from a nightmare." – Alfred Hitchcock

"All right, thanks!" she said, and went inside.

Ungowa, thought Harry.

But now he had lost sight of the crane again!

What was he to do!

He went to the bar to talk to some people.

He asked them: "Hey, you guys, I'm looking for the base of a red and white crane. And they said "why don't you just teleport there!" and Harry responded "I've never been there before! I can only teleport places I've been!" and they said "why don't you just try teleporting to a place near where it is," and Harry said "I'm afraid, man," with a smile on his face, and both parties, Harry and they, realized that Harry really didn't care about finding the base of the crane, that he really just wanted to talk to people and attain that feeling of unconscious ease one receives in fellowship with others. But Harry and they would never admit this to one another. No, it was a tacit understanding which both parties respected, because they valued the importance of autonomy and self-reliance in society. Harry really didn't have that much to do, you see. As he blazed a golden trail to the top of the independent movie-theatre business and attained the goals he identified himself with, he realized that in the society he operated in, he needed to fashion more goals for himself if he ever wished to receive the attention and love which was the object of his inner, primal goal.

So he gave to charity, expressed himself through drawing, poetry, music, and selecting clothes, going skiing, mountain biking, motocrossing, windsurfing, sky diving...and becoming curious about the mysteries of the world around him and bringing those mysteries to the forefront of his mind and forever perpetuating the mystery by following his desires.

Astrofox

Astrofox went to the movies with his new hubbie, Junebug Jersey. He'd had a crush on her for a year and she'd had a crush on him for a week. In his Astrotruck, Astrofox had a box of 1000 spores. Halfway through the movie, he planned to impregnate mizz junebug with them. There were a whole slew of hilarious gugwappers prancing into the movie theater when the couple arrived. They paraded through the parkinglot with elephant masks and laser sticks singing a song which went "there pufft the lubdred reeb, massing on the floor/ the horn of looey sang to me, he'd heard his cutey's snar."

In front of the theatre-entrance stood Yazzik ,the man whose job it was to feel the faces of the patrons to see if they were animal or human (many tried to fake genus to get in with their friends). He was a tall man with a wide, white face peopled by pimples which stood out like strawberries against snow. Astrofox had a penchant for moonshine, so while in line, he surreptitiously retrieved a flask from his boxer-briefs and dislodged the skin of his person mask to take a swig. However, in his haste to put the mask back in place, he left a tiny bit of fur visible. When the two came to Yazzik, the tall man scanned Junebug easily (she was a beautiful human after all) and she skipped to the entrance, tentatively awaiting her cute fox friend. She was very anxious to see the film: "Bill the Ball," the story of an anthropomorphic billiard ball and his desire to be the last ball potted at the international Billiards championships, even after the 8-ball, who was named "Necros."

Yazzik ran his hand over Astrofox's mask and found the tiny bit of fur.

"NARG!" exclaimed Yazzik. "Youz not a person. Youz a vermin animal!" And with a terrific grunt, Yazzik tossed Astrofox into the parkinglot. Junebug Jersey was concerned about Astrofox, but she was also anxious not to miss the commercials before the trailers. She liked the commercials. Some people liked the previews or the movie better, but Junebug Jersey liked the commercials. They gave her ideas for things to buy. So with an apologetic look at the crumpled and groaning Astrofox, she joined the throng of gugwrappers and laser sticks and went into the movie theatre without him.

Astrofox and the other animals stood outside, shivering. Yazzik leered at

them blindly from inside the box
office. Yazzik had a radiator next to
him. His wet socks were drying on the
radiator. There was only one screen at
this movie theatre, and in this age of
the epic soliloquy, most of the movies
were 4 or 5 hours. So Yazzik, after
feeling everyone's faces, sat around
picking his thumb for a long time.

Yazzik did not see Astrofox glaring at
him. "Fuck you, fuck you, fuck you,
fuck you, fuck..." said Astrofox under
his breath as he glared at
Yazzik. Astrofox had to get his spores
into the movie theatre, so that
Junebug Jersey would have lots of
Astrobabies. He briefly imagined what
the Astrofox-human babies would look
like. It would be like a human with fox
ears and really cool space-bandit
clothes, thought Astrofox. The babies
would break open Junebug Jersey's
tummy and kill her, but an Astrofox
has gotta do what an Astrofox has
gotta do, in this case continue his

life.

You see, children, an Astrofox is immortal as long as he plants his seed. His soul is transferred to the Astrobabies when they are born. Though Astrofox was only in high school, he was getting close to the end of his natural life. He had to plant those spores soon.

A fox mate would not be killed like a human mate, but Astrofox had to get some human DNA for his next corpus. He had sworn to himself: "never again will an Astrofox be legally spit on or lended to in a predatorial way!"

Astrofox racked his brain for a plan. "Rack, rack, rack," went Astrofox's racking stick on his brain.

The racking stick was made of bamboo, beads, and hemp. The beads and hemp searched the grooves of

Astrofox's brain for clumps of electricity he could make plans out of. After gathering 60 milliliters of electricity, Astrofox made a wish, and one of God's angels emailed a plan directly to his, so to speak, mind's eye.

"Aha!" said Astrofox.

God's plan was simple. All Astrofox had to do was fly his Astrotruck over the theatre-wall and scale down a rope with the spores. The theatre didn't have a ceiling. It was like a cross between a roman coliseum and a theatre. The benches were arranged in a semicircle.

So Astrofox invented the flying car and reformatted his Astrotruck to fit the flying car paradigm and he was set.

He smoothed the shiny steering wheel with his paw. He put more wax on. Then he smoothed the shiny steering-wheel with his paw. Then he

put more wax on. Then he smoothed
the shiny steering-wheel with his
paw. Then, like, more wax. Then,
like, paw. Then wax. Then yeah.
Then Mmm.

He checked to see that he had enough
gas. He didn't. He went to the gas
station to get more. The gas station
was a Conoco gas station. He bought
eclipse spearmint gum in the gas
station. And he also bought gas at the
gas station. He chatted to the
attendant about his plans for the
evening.

"So I got this chick right? And I'm
totally gonna give her my spores..."

"Awesommme..." said the attendant.

Astrofox got in his astrotruck and
drove back to the movie theatre.

Junebug Jersey sat in the third row,
watching Bill make jokes, thinking

about going outside to see how Astrofox was doing. She pulled her jacket around her tightly. She wished there was a warm, fuzzy Astrofox around to keep her warm in the chilly, open-air theatre.

When Astrofox arrived, he found Yazzik sitting on top of the theatre-wall, where the back benches were, presumably guarding against an aerial intrusion of some kind. Yazzik had a highly sophisticated sense of hearing and knew what making a flying car sounded like. All the other rejected animals had left. Astrofox eyed Yazzik from across the parking lot and Yazzik vividly heard the distant rattle of the Astrotruck's carburetor.

"A death match," thought Astrofox.

"when I get home I'm going to break open a box of Kraft macaroni and cheese and I am going to add sour cream and Wolf Brand chili and mozzarella and Chipotle Tabasco sauce to it and it is going to be so delicious," thought Yazzik, before also thinking "a death match."

In a death match players are divided into two teams and the team who makes the other team not alive or as unalive as they can make them wins. Player 1 = Yazzik. Special move: seismic toss. Player 2 = Astrofox. Special move: Truck-ram. Player 1 constitutes team 1, while player 2 and CPU-player Junebug Jersey constitute team 2. Astrofox starts off with a power-ram, revving the engine to 150. He's got terrific acceleration, even in mid-air with his newly invented flying car. Yazzik counters with a forcefield and deflects Astrofox's onslaught. With Astrofox's Astrotruck reeling, Yazzik shoots lasers out of his pimples and melts Astrofox's tires – well john, what do you make of this. Well, Al, Team 2 has all this talent, this flying car, this full tank of gas, this desire to rupture the CPU player's stomach with writhing Astrofox embryos. They've got a good game plan, but they don't have the experience when it comes to Death Matches. You've gotta look at the numbers: Yazzik, 3 and O, Astrofox O and O. Yazzik's killed 3 self-aware creatures in his lifetime. That's what Team 2 is up against. It's new territory. They're like Meriwether Lewis and William Clark making their way through the American badlands, but there are savage Native American tribes out there in the badlands, Al, they need someone, a Sacajawea, to gentrify this adamitic savagery that is the more voluminous Death Match experience of Charlie Yazzik.

Charles was Yazzik's first name. Mr. Madden said Charlie because Charlie is a nickname for people named Charles. If you know a little boy at school named Charles, try calling him Charlie sometime to change things up. It may please him. You never know! Sometimes, if you want friends, you have to risk them not liking you. This is how you make your special friends who stay with you for life.

As Mr. Madden used Yazzik's first name nickname and Charlie prepared to roast Astrofox with his pimple-lasers, Junebug Jersey, who was, by now, bored with Bill's soliloquys, looked up and saw Astrofox's Astrotruck battling Yazzik on the wall. She skipped up the benches to where Yazzik stood. She saw him gathering energy from the sun with his pimples. He was going to kill Astrofox! She rushed up to the box officer and with all her might pushed Yazzik off the roof.

Yazzik

Flailed

His

Arms

And

KER-

Splat.

"Ooh!" said John Madden. "Now that got everyone out of their seats!"

Sure enough, the entire audience had rushed from their seats to the back row to get a look at Yazzik's bloody prone form.

"No more masks!" said one animalian theatergoer.

"He was always such an ugly man!" said a human theatre goer. "I'm happy that I won't have to feel surges of anxiety when I go to the theatre because of Yazzik's ugly mug!"

Astrofox pulled up alongside Junebug Jersey, feeling an intense ardor for the homo sapiens sapiens heroine.

"Baby!" he said. "baby, you saved the day! I thought I was gonna be toast out there...but lo, you saved me...you were my Sacajawea..."
"Three cheers for Junebug Jersey!" said one tall kid with glasses. "hip hip!"

"hooray!" said everybody.

"hip hip" said the tall kid.

"hooray!" said everybody

"hip hip"

Nobody said anything

"hip hip" said the boy again.

There was no response whatsoever.

After Yazzik's death, Astrofox became real friends with Junebug Jersey and decided not to implant her with spores.

He impregnated John Madden instead.

That got everyone out of their seats.

Astrofox Jr.

Astrofox went to the beach. At the beach he wore sunglasses. He thought he looked cool in sunglasses. Just as Astrofox remarked to himself "I look cool in this new pair of sunglasses," a 70 foot tall sealizard emerged from the ocean screaming "RRAAAAAAAAAAAAAAAAARRRRRRRRRR R." Everyone on the beach screamed and cried and ran, except Astrofox. He jumped in his Astrotruck and slammed his foot down on the accelerator pedal, steering his vehicle towards the sealizard. The flying car zoomed into a pressure point on the sealizard's neck. When Astrofox hit the creature, the sealizard let out a squawk and fainted. The coastguard tied up the sealizard and put it in a giant aquarium jail, but not before Astrofox impregnated the sealizard with his spores!

As the coastguard encroached, Astrofox retrieved a giant syringe from the back seat of his Astrotruck, and injected the sealizard with his microscopic progeny.
3 days later, the sealizard died as an Astrofox nymph clawed its way through the creature's tissues and intestines.

And so, Astrofox Jr. was born. Astrofox Jr. loves listening to Buddy Holly and Jerry Lee Lewis. In his opinion, Vivien Leigh is sexually attractive. He has other opinions as well.

He reasons using information he has gathered through experience and through what his dad, Astrofox Sr. tells him. The latter is the reason he reasons that he should wear sunglasses to the beach. The reason is that they are cool.

Astrofox Jr. and Astrofox are walking along the beach together. There they are, see? They're waving! Come on children, say "bye bye Astrofox and Astrofox Jr.!" If another sealizard attacks the shore, you can bet that both will impregnate it.

The Day After Bloomsday

That morning, I got out of bed by dint
of a tired, ironic tone. My mother took
me to my therapy appointment. My
mother brought me home from my
therapy appointment. I did nothing. I
saw things. I heard things. I smelled
things. In a contest to decide which
was the most perceptive of my 5
senses, my sight won 1st place, my
hearing won 2nd place, my sense of
touch came in third, my taste buds got
an honorable mention, and my sense
of smell came in last.

I had a vision of God. He told me his
revised version of the Quoran, but I
hadn't taken my Vyvanse so I only

noticed "don't...don't...don't..."

Nothing else happened. I didn't have work that day, the day after Bloomsday. Bloomsday is June 16th, the day the events in James Joyce's *Ulysses* take place. I have only read the first 1 and a half chapters of Ulysses. I didn't read any Ulysses on Bloomsday, or that day, the day after Bloomsday.

I did masturbate though. That was fun.

My tired, ironic tone carried me on a divan across a desert to the Oasis of Authenticity. In the Oasis of Authenticity, I gave the water a curt nod. I gave each of the banana-trees a curt nod. I sat down at the bar next to the swimming pool.
There were women sitting at the bar. I gave them all curt nods. After ordering a Shiner and sipping the shiner for 4 minutes, I approached

them and told them my feelings the way I told them to my therapist.

I approached "them," the women all at once, as one general thing. I approached the sacred essence which binds all women and all of humanity. The sacred essence shimmering in between them, like emotionally stimulating fantasies. The shimmering looked like emotionally stimulating fantasies because it was an emotionally stimulating fantasy. God floated down from heaven to the barstool next to me and continued to recite his revised version of the Quoran.

I left the Oasis. I walked across the desert. I walked across the desert to Dublin. There were so many people and feelings and literature in Dublin. I felt really stupid. I walked for 1 and a half chapters before teleporting back to the last pokemon center I visited.

There, my tired, ironic tone was restored to full health.

I spent the rest of the evening navigating between porn and deviantart. When I achieved orgasm or received a positive comment on one of my stories, I experienced non-ironic feelings and died.

When I died, I went to heaven. And you know what the best thing about heaven is?

You can eat as much as you want and never get fat.

Topher's Fucked Up Moustache

On Wednesday morning, Topher fucked up his moustache. It didn't look fucked up, so he stopped fiddling with it.

At work though, he kept touching his moustache, feeling the patch between the rest of the moustache and the clean-shaven area near his nostrils that, though dark with hair, was a millimeter shorter than the rest of the moustache, seeming more stubbly. He went to the bathroom during his break and looked in the mirror, imagining his moustache without the trompe l'oeil effect of the fucked up portion. What he imagined made him shudder with preemptive embarrassment.

However, he completed his shift, went home, killed one fruit fly with his index finger and went to sleep. As he slept, the mediatory plane between the fucked up portion of the moustache and Topher's nasal cavity sprouted black dots of hair.
The black dots of hair blended with the fucked up portion and Topher, in the bathroom the next morning, found that the black dots exposed his moustache for the fucked up fake it was.

So while he tended his fucked up moustache, Topher allowed himself to be careless and shaved off a rather significant bit. This was the excuse he had been waiting for to shave his moustache and beard completely and not deal with the responsibility facial hair entailed.

As Topher hoovered his face with the

electric razor, he thought "I'll look less awful when I cry without a beard or a moustache."

One week later, Topher went to work hungover. At work he quietly informed a coworker that he had been drinking the night before. The coworker said "Wow! Topher!" and informed everyone, including a girl Topher liked, that Topher had gone to a strip club the night before.

Another coworker said that it was so weird when Topher did things like that because he was so innocent and nice.

The first coworker asked Gina, the girl Topher liked, if she found innocence sexy. Gina said that innocence, on the contrary, was not sexy and, in fact, repellant.

The coworkers joked about Gina being a stripper. Gina laughed. They said Topher should take Gina. "She wants it, Topher," they said.

"Yeah, Topher" said Gina, "you should take me!"

Topher could not bear it and walked quickly away from the counter, through the kitchen, down the hall, to the empty break room. He sat down in one of the blue plastic chairs. He stared at the wall, anger and embarrassment welling up inside him.

Michael, one of Topher's coworkers looked for the mop in the closet across the hall and heard Topher say, by himself, "don't treat me like a fucking animal." Michael thought it was very funny and told the rest of the staff.

The next day Topher had a pimple on his moustache.

He imagined conversations with people he never talked to. He wore a rubber band, and every time he imagined having a conversation with someone, he removed the rubber band from one wrist to the other.

He also had allergies and talked like Billy Bob Thornton in the movie "Slingblade."
The sequence of events that day was thus: get up, shave, talk like Billy Bob Thornton in "Slingblade," brush teeth, check email, masturbate, dress, catch bus, catch train, walk to work, work, come home, kill self.

When Topher killed himself he went to the Afterworld of Fuckedupmoustacheland. Everybody in Fuckedupmoustacheland had a fucked up moustache too.

Topher's appraisal of the people of Fuckedupmoustacheland was that they were all very self-absorbed. During his stay in Fuckedupmoustacheland, he cultivated a kind-but-wise facial expression, the facial expression he remembered Morgan Freeman having in "Shawshank Redemption."

He also ate a lot – because, as we all know, the best thing about being in heaven is that you can eat as much as you want and never get fat.

The Sheep With No Brain

The sheep had no brain.

Its only friend was a little boy named Sam.

Sam liked to mess with the sheep.

Sam would say the sheep was a good sheep when it was just being its sheep-self, but when the sheep became confident and tried to do something cool, Sam would say the sheep was a dumbass.

The sheep tried to act naturally, which it thought could best be achieved by being quiet and staring at itself on the inside of its irises.

The sheep tried to laugh at Sam's jokes in a way it thought would be deemed socially acceptable.

The sheep hated itself.

The sheep liked Sam, but tried to stay away from Sam, so as not to make Sam think that the sheep liked him too much.

The sheep stayed indoors playing NFL Madden 2005 and sticking to the tenets of the religion Makeyerbedevrymorningism.

The sheep neglected to tend to its basic social skills so that when it talked its voice cracked and when it thought to ask a question the questions were about armhair and the taste of vaginal fluid.

Eventually the sheep converted from

Makeyerbedevrymorningism to Baseidentityonnotbeinggoodenough ism.

One day, when the sheep met some new people who weren't Sam for the first time in a while, the sheep was revolted by the fact that the only thing it could talk about was how it struggled to avoid depression.

That was it.

That was the sheep.

"BAAAAAAAAAAAAAAAAAAAAAAAAAAAAA
AAAAAAAAAAAAAAAAAAAAAAAAAAAAAA
AAAAAAAAAAAAAAAAAAAAAAAAAAAAAA
AAAAAAAAAAAAAAAAAAAAAAAAAAAAAA
AAAAAAAAAAAAAAAAAAAAAAAAAAAAAA
AAAAAAAAAAAAAAAAAAAAAAAAAAAAAA
AAAAAAAAAAAAAAAAAAAAAAAAAAAAAA
AAAAAAAAAAAAAAAAAAAAAH!"
mourned the sheep.

The sheep felt exhausted from

mourning and ordered a pizza.

When the pizza arrived 30 minutes later, it made the sheep feel good.

The sheep shared its pizza with the television and felt double-plus good.

The sheep had no brain.

It stared at the empty pizza box with no brain and therefore no brain-electricity and therefore no ideas.

"Fuck me," said the sheep. "Fuck me for not having any idea.

The Premeditatedly Conceived Art Object

The Premeditatedly-Conceived Art-Object walked into Starfucks Coffee and stood in line.

4 of the 7 people working in this Starfucks had a tattoo. 3 of those 4 people got their tattoos while in college. The Starfucks employee who hadn't gotten his in college received his when he was 8 years old. This employee's name was Scott. The tattoo Scott received when he was 8 covered his entire back. The tattoo depicted three Velociraptors running. If the tattoo were a theatre

production, the Velociraptors would be running in the direction of stage-left.

The middle Velociraptor had a thought bubble above his head that read "timor omnis abesto."

In latin, "timor omnis abesto" translates as "all fear be absent."

Nobody could see Scott's tattoo because he was wearing a Starfucks work-shirt.

If the tattoo were a theatre production, it would be called Deinonychus: The Journey Begins. In the play, the middle Velociraptor, Damien, distinguished from the others by a horn on his forehead, would grow up in a peaceful, Ornithomymus-ruled kingdom. Unable to understand his thirst for blood growing up in the gentle herbivorous community, Damien would feel depressed and alienated. However, on his 7th birthday a giant, fat Velociraptor named Simon would arrive and tells Damien that he was a Carnivore, and that there was a whole galaxy of animals like him outside of the Ornithomymus kingdom. Damien would go to a special boarding school for Velociraptors called "Deinonychus State," (D-State in the student-vernacular). There, he would meet the other two Velociraptors in the tattoo, clumsy, good natured Ryan, and his bookish, sarcastic love interest, Jo-lee.

The Premeditatedly-Conceived Art-Object waited in line for 5 minutes before premeditatedly buying a "tiny" coffee. The sizes at Starfucks are a little confusing for youngly acquainted patrons. The smallest drink you can get is a "tiny," the second largest size you can get is a "short," and the largest drink you can get is a "regular." The Premeditatedly-Conceived Art-Object had a lengthy track-record with Starfucks. He had come to Starfucks every morning for the last 5 years.

When the Premeditatedly-Conceived Art-Object came to Starfucks, he liked to buy a tiny coffee, settle down on a nice comfortable stool, and read the sports page, a copy of which he usually found discarded nearby.

When he bought his "tiny" coffee from Scott, the Premeditatedly-Conceived Art-Object found no available stool or sports page in the lounge. The Premeditatedly-Conceived Art-Object chose to interpret this unexpected absence of stools and sports-pages as a sign from God that he should use his usual Starfucks-time to appreciate nature. So he went for a walk.

The Premeditatedly-Conceived Art-Object sipped his tiny coffee as he walked along the building's perimeter, trying to focus his attention on the natural beauty of the trees lining the sidewalk. He thought to himself that the sunlight shining through the trees' branches as they swayed in the wind was beautiful. The Premeditatedly-Conceived Art-Object struggled to find other beautiful things. Clouds proportionate to sky. A grackle's funny mating dance. A squirrel's spasmodic tail-waving. There wasn't much else. He finished his coffee and thought with mustered optimism "it's refreshing to begin your day with exercise."

After his walk, the Premeditatedly-Conceived Art-Object got in his car and drove to work. His job was to draw conclusions about information his bosses sent him. It was easy and paid well.

However, at the end of his workday, the easiness of the Premeditatedly-Conceived Art-Object's well-paying job was not enough to make him happy. In the car going home, the

Premeditatedly-Conceived Art-Object felt sad because he found his social life unsatisfying. He wanted a group of friends and a girlfriend who liked him as much as he liked her. But instead, he had no friends and spent most of his time at home, watching TV.

Because of this discrepancy between his desires and the way he conducted his life, the Premeditatedly-Conceived Art-Object felt terribly alone.

He drank lots of alcohol by himself on a regular basis.

Unattractive deposits developed in his bathroom.

When the Premeditatedly-Conceived Art-Object felt really bad, he prayed to God for the strength to fulfill his commitments and concentrate on the present moment. He also thanked God for what he had, because he believed saying "thank you" made him more grateful.

"Thank you, God," he said through tears, "Thank you, God, for the gift of life. Thank you for nature. Thank you for keeping my body safe from physical harm today. Thank you for my job..."

Giving thanks to God made him feel better. But only a little bit.

Some nights he thought of committing suicide, but when he considered it practically, and knew he didn't have the courage, he calmed down and resolved to take better care of himself.

Then, the next day, he would make a joke or listen to someone.

But then he'd feel sad again.

The Premeditatedly-Conceived Art-Object writhed in a whirlpool of feeling sad and resolving to feel better and feeling sad and resolving to feel better for months more. And finally, one day, he'd felt sad again one too many times. The Premeditatedly-Conceived Art-Object killed himself.

When he entered the land of the dead through its black archway which said "Timor Omnis Abesto," and saw all the other ghosts walking around or milling in groups of 3 to 8, the Premeditatedly Conceived Art Object began to ask himself repeatedly the two questions he always asked himself when entering a social situation:
1. Am I better, or worse looking than this person?
2. Am I more, or less intelligent than this person?

Badger 3's Use of Falcon Punch

There were three badgers who lived in a gingerbread house. Their favorite singer was the big bopper. When the big bopper died in Buddy Holly's Plane Crash, the badgers were sad and punched holes in the walls of their gingerbread house.

"Falcon punch," said one of the badgers when he punched through.

The other two badgers laughed when this happened. Releasing their pleasureprinciple/anger tension through laughter, the badgers felt better about themselves, but badger 3 who had said "Falcon Punch" without irony, attempting to use the statement made by Captain Falcon in the popular videogame super smash bros. as a way of emphasizing his pleasureprinciple/anger tension to his peers, felt sad. He was only trying to be poetic. But he was a bad poet and he failed.

There are many awful poets out there in the wide world of sports. The awful poets become very emo when they realize how awful they are. And after the period of emo comes the period of nothingness. and after the nothingness comes the period of ensuing happiness.

The happiness ensues around the nothingness. The nothingness is like a shiny white pebble and the happiness is reality touching it.

Badger 3 touched himself many times after being laughed at. Many times. He had 6 okay to cringingly awful and traumatizing sexual experiences. But he mainly just touched himself.

He used Falcon Punch to fight the emo feelings he had about his awful poetry.

He ate over 100 Queso and Steak Burritos from Qdoba. 117 to be precise.

One day he came home to the ginger bread house, that only he lived in now, and wrote down everything: the past, the present, the future, details, ideas, whimsies.

When he'd written everything, he came to 3 conclusions:
1. His greatest levels of happiness had occurred in fantasies of talking to women he never talked to.
2. he had to buy and read every comic book by Daniel Clowes.
3. Surreal stories that exercised his imagination were crucially important

and that getting into literature for the past year had made him forget how crucially important surrealism was to his spiritual diet.

He licked his pen and said "damn" in an affected ghetto way.

In the graph of his life there were new X and Y coordinates: X was now designated by "Surreal Stories" and Y by "Time"

Badger 3 sat down in the middle of the floor saying "God Bless America" in various Afro-American intonations. He then started singing "y'all gon make me lose my mind/ up in here, up in here" as he concocted a story about Barack Obama visiting Narnia and making everyone on board the Dawn Treader a delicious fruit salad.

The Bug, The Bird, And The Link

The bug had cats for toes.

The bird had cats for a nose.

So the bug and the bird made a link.

They went to the park with their link. "Hey," said a boy.

"Hey," said the bug and the bird.

The boy grinned and nodded "nice link."

The bug and the bird chortled.

They went to the store and bought a warm bag to have their link in together.

Next, they went for a walk.

Next, they went for a fly.

The cats made lots of noise, at first, in the air.

Next, they bought a cottage.

"and you can smell the vines touching the mailbox," said the bug to the bird.

"and you can feel the sea go on and on like it's watching over your ears," said the bird

And the sea collapsed, lovingly collapsed outside as the bug sang songs to the bird.

And the bird sang songs to the bug.

The cats sang songs to each other and made more cats.

The new cats plopped from the link like pears into water.

"like pears into water," said the bird.

"like pears into water," said the bug.

"remember reality?" said the bird.

"yes," said the bug, "reality never felt like pears into water. reality was not nice. no one liked my writing. i was afraid to talk about my writing with anyone, even though it was the only thing i cared about."

"hmm," said the bird, "i remember one time in reality when my stomach made a noise in science class and everyone looked around because it was so loud and i was red and my belt was tight on my tummy and my pants were already tight and i'd had french fries and ranch dressing for lunch and the girl i liked sat one seat ahead and to the right of me and i wanted to leave and i remember in reality i left class all the time because i felt so overwhelmingly self-conscious that i felt like i was gonna cry even though no one was paying attention to me so i went to the bathroom for the rest of class and sat against the wall and talked to the other boys when they came in to pee and i wrote song lyrics on the wall."

The bird breathed.

The bug breathed.

The cats shifted.

"i never lived in reality," the bird confessed.

"i never lived in reality," the bug lamented.

The cats shifted.

"i suck," said the bird.

"i suck," said the bug.

"everything sucks," said the bird.

"why can't we have any fun?" said the bug.

"what is fun?" said the bird.

"something we can't have," said the bug.

The sea collapsed, lovingly collapsed outside.

"i doubt myself," said the bird.

"i don't understand what anybody says to me," said the bug.

The sea collapsed, lovingly collapsed outside.

The sea collapsed and collapsed and collapsed. There came a storm.

The cottage flew into the storm, turning upside down and around.

The bird flapped his wings inside the flying cottage.

"reality sucks," said the bug.

"reality sucks," said the bird.

"i suck," said the bug.

"i suck," said the bird.

The sea collapsed, lovingly collapsed.

The vine held onto the mailbox.

"even though you suck and i suck, i love you," said the bug.

The bird was very busy.

The bug shouted again.

The bird narrowly avoided a flying bag of catfood.

So the bug shouted again: "even though...you suck...and i suck...i love you."

"i love you too!" said the bird, furiously flapping his wings in the gale.

"we should still say 'yes' to life, even though everything sucks, right?"

The bird did not answer. The bird was very tired.

"we should still say 'yes' to life," hollered the bug, "am I right, or am I right?"

The bird had no choice, he guessed, but his nose meowed and felt warm when he found the window and soared out.

I Don't Want To Do Anything

A fat man sat next to a fat
woman. They sat on blossom-pods on
the cement above a storm drain. The
fat man was in one of his "moods." He
leaned on the fat woman's breast.

"I don't want to do anything," he said.

"Oh but you have to do things," said
the fat woman, "that's life." She had a
backpack on her lap. Both had
backpacks. Both walked around a lot
because they did not have cars.

"No I don't," said the fat man.

"Yes, you do. You have to work,"

"No, I just want to stay here," said the fat man, sitting up. "If I need food, or shelter, or anything, I'll get up, but right now I don't want anything so I don't want to."

The fat woman was quiet.

The ground had rain all over it. They had talked in the cemetery earlier. They sat in the cemetery's "foyer," on the blossom-pods now, talking because the fat man had decided that he still needed to be in the cemetery.

"I just want to write children's books," said the fat man. "I've never wanted to do anything. I've only ever done things because I felt like I should do them. All I want to do is write children's books."

The fat woman laughed. "you should do that, then."

"I want to write children's books. And write all about my life. And write lots of bad things about my mom and my dad and my brother-"

"hey," said the fat woman, "your mom seems amazing."

"She's not," said the fat man, "she just always tries to seem amazing. She tries to seem humble, and committed, and caring-" The fat woman punched the fat man.

"Your mom's been there for you," said the fat woman, "don't talk shit about her."

"Well, if she was there for me, I wouldn't have ended up like this."

"That's bullshit!" said the fat woman, "take some responsibility for yourself. We are who we are because of our perceptions and experiences, not just our parents!"

"Well, I don't care," said the fat man. "I'm still gonna talk shit about her, because that's what I wanna do."

The fat woman got up. "I'm going to get some water. You are welcome to come if you want."

The fat man did not respond.

The fat woman shook her head, hoisted her backpack onto her fat shoulders, and walked through the cemetery gates. The fat man laid down in the fetal-position, using his backpack as a pillow

Earlier, the fat man had been shaking violently in the fat woman's arms and he did not know why and he was worried that he might have been abused as a child.

He looked at the blossom tree. "Crate Myrtles,"- was that what they were called? He felt calm. He wondered if he should go to a bar. It was 2 O'clock. He felt like getting drunk and talking to people. He felt lots of complex emotions. He spoke 5 complete sentences to the "Crate Myrtle" and briefly closed his eyes.

Then he got up, and got out his cellphone. He called one friend. No answer. He saw another friend in the contacts list, but then remembered he was at work. Then he called the fat woman, and then he called the fat woman again, and again, and again, and then he called the fat woman again.

3 Ants Beat Up God

3 ants beat up God. They kicked him in the head. Then they rolled him over and punched him in the butt. God became incensed and took out his anger on the Ku Klux Klan, melting all of them in his stomach-lava. God hated everything. He made a hat that said "I hate everything" on it. It was a 1950s sailor-hat and it made him look puerile. People saw his puerile hat and thought "arrested development," and raised their eyebrows.

God did something mean to an animal. The animal cried.

God did something mean to a

fish. The fish cried.

God did something mean to God. God cried.

The ants beat up God again and again in God's memory. He felt vulnerable and lashed out defensively.

"Don't treat me like a fucking anima!" said God to the wall.

Kyle's Film Class

A High School senior named Kyle had a great idea for a short-film. His idea was about a mentally-handicapped boy who happens upon a group of high school girls on their way to volleyball practice. The girls regard the boy with a mixture of condescending sympathy and open mockery. When the girls leave the boy and enter the gym, he gets beaten up by two people for no reason. Then he wakes up and says "Thank you very much," to the camera in an Elvis voice.

Originally, Kyle wanted to do an art film made up of random fleeting moments shot with a variety of characters at various locations all around the school. But the teacher said that the short films had to be about high school students and that they had to use certain lines like "what would Elvis do" and do other creativity-instigating things.

Kyle, his hopes not the least bit dampened by the new constraints, banged out a 4 page script as soon as he got home. He thought his idea was a little unconventional, but with a clear script, complete with filming locations and stage directions, he was confident that the group would acquiesce to the idea based on its organization.

But when he made his pitch, the group said, "nuh-uh," and looked at him weird. Kyle wanted his vision to become a reality and was angry about the group's verdict. He felt he had done everything right, and that the group had chosen Alice's idea because he was socially awkward/weird. He thought his idea was far superior as a work of art. His classmates didn't know anything about film, and besides, they just wanted to do something easy.

Lots of guys had crushes on Alice, even though she was ugly and had an ugly country voice. People seemed to think she seemed okay with who she was, or something.

She dated Kyle's former friend Luke. On Homecoming night, she was changing in the back of Luke's truck and Kyle didn't notice. He had stood there idly, wondering what Alice was doing in the back seat. "Do you mind?" Luke had said sharply.

Kyle had felt embarrassed.

3 years later Kyle felt embarrassed about his behavior in the film class. The film class had said nuh-uh and looked at him weird because he

wanted one kid, Nate, to play the mentally-handicapped guy.

"Why? Do you think I look retarded or something?" Nate had asked. Nate did in fact look a bit strange. He had a small skinny body and a large head. Though he was a Junior he appeared to be a few years younger. Kyle felt the painful realization that Nate might well have been teased for being strange-looking, and that he should have taken this into account.

Kyle's script involved the mentally-handicapped boy being beaten up, which wasn't much of a sell, and also dialogue between girls. Kyle had no close female friends or sisters and didn't really know how teenage girls talked to one another. He thought his script might have seemed awkward to the girls in the group.

TRACY: (Slightly over-effusive) OH! I didn't know you had a boyfriend! What school does he go to?

JENNY: He goes to Lynch. We've been dating for about 2 months.

TRACY: Oh my God Jenny! You should have told mee!

Kyle decided that no one would ever hear of his young career as a screenwriter.

He submerged all memory of the film class in his unconscious mind.

3 days later a mind-bear came to his conscious mind's campsite and he dug up the film class memory to scare the bear away. As the bear grew a second pair of arms and advanced, Kyle brandished the memory before him like Christ's shield and felt great whooshes of pain as the bear's arms and extra-arms mauled his memory to bloody silver ribbons. He cried out in agony.

He was shaken at first but then took a shower and relaxed in front of his laptop with a cold PBR and watched Arrested Development.

"Pretty soon, I'm gonna get out of my own Arrested Development," he thought.

Kyle liked that Maebe called Lucille Bluth "Gengie." He found nung-nung sounds pleasant.

A giant robot made synthesizerish nung-nung sounds as it passed Kyle's window. "ohhhh yeah..." said Kyle like the cartoon character Garfield sinking into a hot tub. Kyle's ears were having a good day with all this nung nunging. His ears were having such a good day that he thought it was a good day to go punch god in the face for letting him develop irregularly in early childhood.

"Fuck you, God," said Kyle to God's crumpled body. He kicked God and broke one of his ribs. "That's for Daniel Johnston," he said. Then, he kicked God in the face, breaking God's nose. "and that's for Chris-Chan."

Kyle poured beer on God's face.

The dark room Kyle left God's dead body in was hot and moist. Luminous, electric blue fungi bloomed from God's Orifices

Driving Us To The Acid House

Charles Bukowski, Richard Brautigan, and Irvine Welsh sat on Gerald's bed, sun-tanning because Gerald had rented the sun for the weekend. Gerald, Charles Bukowski, Richard Brautigan, and Irvine Welsh were all so happy with their lovely sun. Elsewhere on the planet, human beings cried and died of frostbite. Soon however, they would not be crying, for Gerald had to take the sun back at 12 AM Monday morning and it was eleven thirty and the clock was jumping, jumping.

"After we take the sun back, we should go chill at my Acid House," said Irvine

Welsh.

"What's an Acid House?" said Charles Bukowski.

"Is it a house made out of Acid, or is it a house where people do Acid?" asked Richard Brautigan.

"It's a house made out of Acid where we play music called Acid House," said Irvine Welsh. "Y'all should come on, and bring your jukebox money."

Richard Brautigan and Charles Bukowski looked tentatively at Gerald. Gerald stared at an empty beer bottle on his desk.

"Gerry," said Richard Brautigan, "Gerry, is it okay if Charles Bukowski and I spend the night at Irvine Welsh's Acid House...I know you can't go because you have work tomorrow, but would it be okay if you just took us..."

Gerald stared at the beer bottle. His lips were taut, his expression stern. Nobody in the room said anything. Then, Irvine Welsh said "we'll be the only warm people on the planet when we go outside. It'll be weird."

"Yes," said Richard Brautigan. "That is a true statement."

Nobody spoke for a while.

Then, Gerald said "okay, I'll take you guys over there. I've got plenty of time. I was spending all of that time calculating how much time I had and I realized that I've got plenty."

"Sweet," said Richard Brautigan.

"Yeah," said Charles Bukowski.

"You're a very loving person, Gerald," said Irvine Welsh.

Jerky

Nia, Robert, and Gerry were standing around the Host-stand. Gerry had a crush on Nia. He tried not to pay attention to her, because paying too much attention to someone he had a crush on made him more nervous around them.

Nia was peeling the skin off of her thumb. She asked Robert if he wanted some Nia-jerky. She meant her dead thumb-skin. Robert smiled at her in a way that said *that's a clever joke and I find it funny but I would never, ever think you were being serious*.

Then, Nia turned to Gerry.

"How about you?" she said "Want some Nia-jerky?"

Gerry said "um" and smiled, not knowing what to say.

Nia laughed. "Ha! You're thinking about it! That's great: you were actually thinking about it!"

Gerry blushed. "No..." he said. Customers walked up to the host-stand and Robert ripped their tickets.

Gerry was upset the next day and went to the thanksgiving chapel in Downtown Dallas to ask God to help him not to pay attention to Nia.

While doing this, he behaved in a histrionic way.

4 ladies entered the chapel and sat down. After about 4 minutes, in a hoarse, histrionic voice Gerry asked

the ladies as one "do you pray?"

"yes," said a chubby lady in a purple shirt with short gray hair.

"how do you pray?" Gerry asked, leaning forward with his elbows on his knees, and when the lady answered Gerry nodded and said "gotcha."

The ladies were there for 10 minutes and then they left.

When they left, Gerry wished they hadn't seemed annoyed. He wished they'd thought he was cool.

Igor

Igor read Ghostworld on the train. He giggled at something Enid said. He looked up to see if anybody had reacted to his giggle. No cigar.

Igor got off the train at Zambingo Community College. He walked across the platform to 7-11. The 7-11 cashier glared at Igor and Igor tried to appear extra-cheerful when he asked for two jalepeno cream cheese taquitos. As he walked out of the 7-11, Igor accidentally let the door close on a man in a wheelchair. "I'm a bad boy," thought Igor's inner child. He finished both taquitos in 15 seconds. "hot dog," said Igor.

Igor went to the library to read Ghostworld because he didn't want to talk to the autistic kid in his class. He didn't like the autistic kid because his social awkwardness reminded Igor of himself. Igor spent 15 minutes digesting 10 pages of Ghostworld and 3 chapters of Barry Gifford's "Sad Stories of the Death of Kings." He looked up now and again at the people filing through the library. "Not-Friend" said Igor's inner child, "Not-Friend."

Igor went to the bathroom before class. 9:27. He had 3 minutes to auto-erotically asphyxiate himself.

At 9:30, Igor emerged from the bathroom. "Mission accomplished," he said to himself, smiling.

The autistic kid said hello. Igor nodded and beamed at the autistic kid.

The teacher arrived and everyone filed in. Igor took out his notebook. "fuck everybody," thought Igor. Igor had a cowlick in his hair today and he was sweaty from autoerotically asphyxiating himself. Such conditions incited a certain response in Igor. "Sweat...cowlick," thought Igor. "sweat...cowlick...sweat...cowlick...sweat...COWLICK!"

Igor stood up and took off his shirt. The class gasped and gasped more as Igor ran around the classroom singing "I am the bravest pigeon! I have the prettiest eggs!"

"Igor does not know anything," said the teacher. "This is how someone who hates life behaves - by ruining it for everyone else."

Igor ran from the room. Outside, he took off his shoes and jeans and made a *grand jetee* across the 600 hall.

The Good Will

In the deepest caverns of hell, once upon a time there was a fat dirty bunny that ate towels. He liked to c-walk between Deep Cavern A and Deep Cavern B. It was good practice. He implemented c-walking to Deep Cavern B into his daily routine so that after about a month he did it automatically. "Automatic," he thought and also "swish," as he watched his body seamlessly transition to c-walk mode.

He c-walked in a zig-zag, c-walking on his left foot on the zig and the right foot on the zag. c-walking in this formation pleased him because it reminded him of when he was a clean bunny on the surface and enjoyed sail-boating. When one wants to go straight into the wind on a sailboat, one tacks in a zig-zag. The bunny wasn't c-walking with the wind though. He was c-walking in a zig zag so that both of his feet were balanced skill-wise. He was giving himself his own wind.

Satan thought this was good for the bunny. "He has a goal," thought Satan.

Each week, the bunny rewarded himself for keeping up with his c-walk routine by eating a whole bunch of towels in Deep Cavern B. Now, the bunny always ate a whole lot of towels when he c-walked to Deep Cavern B, but on this weekly anniversary he ate a whole whole lot. So much that he almost overgrazed. He pushed the towel supply of Deep Cavern B, but he always left a little bit of towel culture that respawned quite fast, so it was okay.

When he learned to c-walk he would have the satisfaction of knowing how to c-walk, which was enough for him. The bunny had few desires and they were simple ones, or so he thought he thought and said.

He desired the touch of a girl bunny. That's for sure.

But when you're just eating towels in the Deepest Caverns of Hell, you forget, or rather you make yourself forget about your desire to be touched. Because you can't make somebody touch you. They have to want to touch you. This is a good thing, a very good thing. But it makes some people sad in a weird way where they don't think of themselves as being sad but are very sad all the time. The bunny's mind was a bubble of sadness. A bubble with opaque walls. The bunny's hidden agenda with his C-walk routine was to hopefully woo a girl bunny with his skills at a club or a party some day.

Sometimes he'd ask other bunnies in hell, "hey, what's up?" and they'd say "hey" and he'd say "you guys want to hang out?" and they never did except sometimes and those times he suddenly remembered that he had a lot of things to do and noticed that the bunnies who were like "yeah, dude, totally," could possibly have character flaws and this was the bubble of sadness that he was trapped in.

But he had towels.
He had towels and he never, ever overgrazed. And he kept things going like this his entire life.

At the 75% mark of his life, he looked back at all his memories and shrugged and said "call it a life," and wasn't convinced but went on doing things the way he did them anyway.

At the end of his life, you wouldn't believe how well he could c-walk...it was club-promoter-worthy. At the 75% mark, when he was unconvinced, something happened to his nerve endings. He couldn't feel his nerve-endings. They were burning. The pain was so great. He prostrated himself against the wall of Deep Cavern A and screamed and shouted and no one heard him and he screamed and shouted more and he opened his eyes and he continued to do things the same way, like I said, until the end of his life, but he kind of lived, y'know, and he was very polite and things were simpler and he didn't worry about girls.

And a girl bunny named Sarah fell into hell one day and he helped her up and licked her scabbed knees with his soothing bunny tongue even though he was sort of embarrassed to because she was a girl.

She didn't rebuke him. Her knees healed and she was grateful and they were friends and it turned out she didn't mind hanging out with him even if he was in a bubble of sadness and so he taught her how to c-walk and she showed him how to do other stuff like shuffle.

He knew he was in love with her, but didn't know how to love her from within his bubble of sadness.
But they kept meeting each other for their respective dance lessons and things eventually worked out.
The bubble of sadness was always there, but they found ways of tacking around it.

The bubble of sadness never goes away in any of us. This seems so hopeless even when you tack around it! It works better if you re-write the story.

There was a bunny. He struggled at
first, but he didn't struggle after a
while and he was thankful for what he
had and enjoyed his time in hell.
And after Sarah came into his life this
second story was much more
true. The bunny had everything he
needed. But what about the
romance? The action? The
adventure? It was there. The
kingdom of Heaven was there in Hell
as well as on Earth.

You cannot break the bubble of
sadness, no matter the extent of the
austerities you put yourself
through. Be polite and try to do
good. Be grateful for what you
have. Doing that will not make the
bubble of sadness go away, but it will
change your perception of things so
that you don't focus on it, or I mean
you will focus on it, it just won't be the
guest on 60 minutes week after week
after week after week, I don't know,

stomp all of this earnestness into the ground, push your body to its limits, interact with lots of people, listen to everything, eat towels, eat towels tomorrow, plan your entire week of eating towels, plan your entire month of eating towels, learn to c-walk, don't learn to c-walk, c-walk badly, pretend to be learning to c-walk in your imagination, attempt to c-walk while imagining you are learning to c-walk even though you don't think you will ever learn to c-walk properly, have a c-walk routine, tell people you have a c-walk routine even though you maybe c-walk once a week for 15 minutes even though you tell yourself you c-walked for half an hour, torture yourself endlessly with your awareness that you are desperately afraid of eating the last vestiges of the towel-culture and being without towels in Deep Cavern B even though you eat so many towels that you should be ravenous and far-gone enough to eat the last vestiges of towel culture

without thinking and are only eating
the towel supply down to its nubbins
because in the deepest caverns of your
mind you want a girl bunny to touch
you and feel sympathy for a towel-
eater who is in such a pathetic bind
and how you feel this is the only way
your bubble of sadness will go away
but you are always too afraid of
creating that much of a problem in
your life even though your life already
sucks. *I shall go on in the same way,
losing my temper with Ivan the
coachman, falling into angry
discussions, expressing my opinions
tactlessly; there will be still the same
wall between the holy of holies of my
soul and other people, even my wife; I
shall still go on scolding her for my
own terror, and being remorseful for
it; I shall still be as unable to
understand with my reason why I
pray, and I shall still go on praying;
but my life now, my whole life apart
from anything that can happen to me,
every minute of it is no more*

meaningless, as it was before, but it has the positive meaning of goodness, which I have the power to put into it.- Tolstoy

Mary, Queen of Cats

Mary was rich, but bored. She qualified for the Olympics and won a gold medal for being bored.

Bored.

Bored.

Bored.

So she decided, as a birthday present to herself, that she would use her money to buy one-hundred cats to reanimate her moribund life.

Mary owned a large house with one-hundred rooms. Each cat was given its own room, complete with litter tray, food dispenser, and a giant foam pillow to sleep on. The cats were the happiest cats in America, and now, Mary no longer felt bored because she could study the cats' behavior. She watched them mill about the stairs, play, fight, and scratch up all of Mary's expensive furniture.

She gave each cat a number in her notes, like so:
"56 and 24 contended over territory next to the grand piano, which, I gather, appears to belong to 24 to start with. But history tells us 56 does not take no for an answer. He is a so-to-speak bull cat. At dinnertime he eats his herring faster than any of the other kitties – except, of course, 72 whose size suggests an ocelot or cougar in his geneaology."

On and on, just like that, went Mary's notes.

Mary observed how after the losing cats suffered injuries, they were not seen as often. When she sought them out, they ceased their frantic licking of scratches and limping and began to leap about again like happy kitties.

"A cat will not let you know when it is hurt," Mary read in an article on the World Wide Web. The article was published on the world's first cat-website. Mary thought herself very modern, clacking the keys of her Computron unit. It was the year 1908 – not many computers existed and the World Wide Web was still in its tadpole stage.

Out of all the cats, number 72 was the mega-bull. He made the most kittens with his cat-penis too. The other cats were afraid of him. Mary began locking the doors of the weaker cats at night because she was afraid 72 would eat them. Still most of the cats were so afraid that they did not come out during the day. The cat-opolis of Mary's dreams that had shielded her from her boredom for so many months was reduced to one large cat lounging in the middle of the lobby, his tail gracefully oscillating like a pendulum. The state of affairs continued for months until Mary decided what she was going to do.

The last entry in her notebook read:

"I have reached the point where I no longer care. The minutes, hours, and days flow out of a gray opacity, make a studied lap around the ballroom and flow back into the mist from whence they came."

Mary took a broom and smashed 72 in the head. 72 spat and hissed and Mary bludgeoned him in the nose. He ran away, squeaking. The few cats who had ventured out to watch the confrontation ran away too and Mary followed with the broom. She did not

wish to hurt the cats; she just wanted
to let them know she was the boss.

Mary disrobed and rolled around gaily
on the marble floor of the lobby. She
shaved her head and all of the hair on
her body. Mary was now queen of the
cats.

She bit and played and used her
advantages as a human to always get
the upper-hand. When she went into
the cats rooms, they were her rooms,
not the rooms she had bought with the
steeply inclined curve of her
computron shares.
And speaking of her steeply rising
stock, the stock was always getting
steeper as talk of war spread across
the United States of America.

At this point in time, Prussia had a
moon colony and vehicles which could
burrow undetected, through the
earth's crust, resurfacing
anywhere. The U.S.A. needed the

potentials of computron if Prussia was to attack.

Meanwhile, Mary's own computron unit lay untouched. She cut the phones, locked the doors. Years passed. Mary was happy. As happy as the 17th century's mountain men who sang songs and killed Indians and explored this country's luscious body on the backs of tall-eared jack-asses.

One day, as we all know, the Prussian Tunnelships came. When one broke ground near Mary's large house, a scout party of the Prussian Navy came and battered down the door.
And there they found Mary and the cats. What ensued was a great battle which the Prussians won, but not without casualties. Mary and several of her subjects fled to the woods and to this day they have not been found, not even in the form of a corpse. She was 37 years old at the time, should be 47 now.

You children should not allow yourselves to be bored, and you should not be surprised by it either. You are bored because of Prussian school, Prussian books, Prussian World Wide Web, and Prussian pop stars singing songs on the radio. When you are bored, create something. You will be able to live inside your own beautiful world.

What We Talk About When We Talk About The Satanic Spaceship Orbiting Earth

I opened the door to find a chicken on
my front porch. I told Jane we'd
gotten another one. She said "yay!"
and jumped up and down. We rushed
outside and I picked up the chicken
and threw it in the driveway. Jane
kicked it against the garage
door. Then I kicked it against the
garage door. We had a super-duper-
fun time kicking the chicken against
the garage door. Then we got in our
Mitsubishi Eclipse and ran over the
chicken. Pink Crystals of chicken-flesh
stuck in the grooves of the tire. We

had to clean that up. Running over the chicken sure was fun though. Jane and I got on the garage floor and ate what was left of the chicken.

"God has blessed us on this day. Praise Jesus!" said Jane
"Mmm-hmm," I said.

But then, all of a sudden, a man-sized monkey of evil fell from the sky. Jane and I got up. We got in our Sephun Sebei Kung Fu stances. The monkey was a minion of Satan, sent from the Satanic Spaceship orbiting earth. I quickly texted my friend Anson for back-up. Anson was my friend as much as the evil monkey was my friend-in-reverse.

"Come to mess with us, monkey?" said Jane

"It's a test ma'am, and I'm today's test-monkey."

"Bring it on, Jimmy John," I said.

The monkey attacked with a ferocious monkey-tornado kick. I countered with a psi-shield. Jane stepped to one side and attempted to slice the Monkey's achilles heel, but missed. The Monkey bounced off my psi-shield and hit a tree-branch. Then he got up and threw a fireball at Jane who was caught unawares. The fireball vaporized her hand. She screeched at the sky and buckled down on her knees. But just then, Anson arrived and suckerpunched the monkey in the back of the head. I finished the monkey off by drawing its lifeforce into my power-ring, but this was little comfort to us. Jane was now right-handless and bleeding and lying in the driveway in the fetal position, crying. Anson and I got her in the Eclipse and headed to the hospital like a couple of Secretariats on meth.

"Fucking monkey. Ruining our day," I

said.

"tch" said Anson

"Sometimes I wish the U.S. would use its nuclear bombs to blow Satan out of space."

"The U.S. is a pawn of Satan. Those are Satan's bombs."

"Yeah, but they don't have to be. I mean, sometimes I feel like Satan causes more good than bad in America. It's well and good to have all the money Satan gives us, but it sucks that he can send monkeys down whenever he wants to take us away like trout on a fishing preserve."

"I ain't complaining. It sucks about Jane's hand and all, but think about our lifestyle: we have these houses built by Satan, we have no responsibilities, and we get to sit around all day stapling each others arms and fucking," Anson looked at me, "and you've gotta admit, those power-rings we have are pretty cool."

"Yeah," I conceded, "those power-rings are pretty bad-ass. The other day, Jane and I used our power-rings to turn a tree into a giant squirrel."

Anson chuckled, "that's pretty cool. One time I turned a tree into 20 batman-dwarves."

"Dude, one time I turned a tree into a Caesar salad the size of a house that had trilobites swimming in it."

"Dude, one time, when I was in college, I turned an empty PBR can into a swarm of mosquitos that made whoever they bit happy for the rest of their lives."

"Wish I was at that party," I said, looking at Jane in the backseat. "I really wish Jane was too."

"Why do you think God gives us chickens," said Sister Alberta to our first grade class. Nobody answered. "God gives us chickens so we can kick them and run them over with our cars," said Sister Alberta. "Now what kind of car do you want when you're a grown up?"

I remembered I said I wanted a Ford F250. A Ford F250 is heavy enough to make a chicken squirt 5 feet when you run it over, I imagine.

At the hospital, Jane got her hand regrown at the regrowing station. She smiled and gave me a giant kiss. *Nom nom nom* was the noise the kiss made. Anson watched us kiss, his hand absent-mindedly rubbing his nipple.

We rode home and invited Anson over to orgy-and-bess it with us. Anson brought over his two wives and we had a festival to celebrate another dead monkey, a limb regrown, and another chicken from God's factory farm crushed.

God's factory farm is located in Mississississississippi, where all of the angels live. The angels eat white bread and paint objects white all day. They are unpleasant to be around, by my count. They work all day to kill chickens for us to kick around and they sweat so much they look yellow.

After we were sweaty from fucking, we all used our power-rings to create an enchanting mist in the middle of the living room. Our naked bodies bathed in the titillating light. I smiled and looked at Jane's naked body. She was fatter than Anson's wives, but it was clear that her weight was apportioned in a more pleasing mannner.

She and I fucked like hot mud rising

and falling, and when we do that there are absolutely no problems with the way things are. They will only get telescopically better.

Self, Just Before

Self ate a potato. A baked
potato. Microwave 4 minutes, turn
over, microwave for another 4. Let it
sit when it beeped. Added ranch,
mexican cheese blend, salsa. Self now
happy squirrel.

But then time passed.

Self stared at the wall thinking about
anxiety. Self could think about anxiety
forever. Anxiety over what? Over
whether self should stand up and
perform action or not. Basic, basic
Erickson's 2nd stage stuff.

Reggae on radio. Toots and the

Maytals. Self hurt all over. Why could
self not be another who
cared more about existing?

Self thought: "maybe read book."

Next thought: "go to show, find girl."

Next thought: "don't know if I like
girls, but that might just be the
Sertraline."

Next thought: "Just what should I
do?"

Then: "maybe I should write." Heard
cat scratch the folded up divider laying
against the wall of the small
apartment. Self did not want to hear
the sound of cat scratching.

Self wrote for 15 minutes, then
thought "I am like Kafka, too sensitive
for this world."

Outside in the humidity, the

cloudcover, the mosquitoes, the sleeping buildings, a large shape descended from the sky. Diameter stretched from self's apartment to, self estimates, 4 blocks away.

The object emitted a loud sound. Loud enough to rustle the trees and cause anyone standing outside to cover their ears and scream.

A great red light thundered down and then everyone and Self went away.

Self in creative writing workshop in heaven now.

Self likes writing in heaven, but also enjoys eating, because in heaven you can eat as much as you want and never get fat.

So Many Empires Rose and Fell

Once upon a time there was
nothing. Then a tiny atom
appeared. Then so many things
happened. You just wouldn't believe
how many things. You just couldn't
imagine how many things. The
number of things that happened was
greater than one million, not even in
the same ballpark as a million even, in
fact, even greater than the greatest
number that anyone has given a name
to, which is Google.

Now, I know when I say Google you
inevitably think about the thing you go
to to search for stuff, but Google is
also the name of this aforementioned

very large number which is even
bigger than a million, and even bigger
than a million millions, even, in fact,
existing in a ballpark that is nowhere
near the ball park a million millions is
in.

So, my point is made: lots of things
have taken place. Numerous events
have occurred. A multiplicity of
happenings have happened. Seas of
happenings. Oceans of
happenings. Little happenings, big
happenings, medium-sized happenings
of any size you could possibly imagine
within the parameters of what you
consider to be a little happening and
what you consider to be a big
happening.

And then. And then what happened?

I'll tell you what happened.

Emily came in the door and announced
that she had done it. She had

splurged half her check on a new pair
of Ray Bahns, which, because she
worked at Sunglass Hut had only cost
her half the listed price.

"Oh my God!" said Shianne, whose
feet were on my lap.

I smiled at Emily and made eye-
contact, trying to judge how effusive a
response this event demanded. I was
already happy to see Emily because
now she was home we could smoke
her pot.
While Emily and Shianne talked
sunglasses and how happy Emily was
that she had bought them and how
boring her shift had been and how
happy she was to be home now, my
gaze alternated between Emily and the
cat. I wished that they would stop
talking so we could smoke Emily's
pot. I stretched my face into happy
shapes. We all stretched our faces
into happy shapes and made various
communicative noises. Then we

smoked pot. Then a whole bunch of other things happened – like, one hundred googles of things and so many more empires rose and fell and so many more happinesses were made.

Blue Moon

Sarah worked in a cake shop. It was slow that day. She leaned against the sink behind the counter with her arms folded. An unattractive, college-y guy was talking to her friend. Sarah tried not to be judgmental. He was probably okay. They were talking about beer. She didn't like beer that much, but she did like Blue Moon. So she thought to say "I like Blue Moon," to contribute something.

"Blue Moon's, like, the beer hipsters who don't know anything about beer drink," said the unattractive college-y guy, laughing. The conversation continued. She felt like a dead astronaut floating in space.

At home that evening she watched Midsomer Murders with her Mom and little half-brother and drank two blue moons and felt like a dead astronaut floating in space. Mainly because she thought she was ugly. She cut up an apple for her half-brother.

Sarah listened to her iPod and texted in bed before going to sleep. She slept 4 hours and then woke up feeling like a dead astronaut floating in space.

She brushed her teeth and listened to her iPod while looking at herself in the mirror for fifteen minutes. 30 minutes later she made an iPod commercial for herself by dancing in the mirror.

On the bus to work, the song "Blue Moon of Kentucky" came on shuffle and she abruptly changed it.

She opened the store with her

manager. She got a drawer. She texted her friend who'd texted her after she'd fallen asleep.

When the morning rush had subsided, she looked at her phone and discovered a text message from the friend that said somebody Sarah had met twice had said she seemed cold.

She couldn't think how anyone would think that about her. But at the same time she feared her worst suspicions were true – that she was an awful, narcissistic person whose every thought perpetuated an intricate matrix of self-deception that prevented her from truly connecting with other people.

For the rest of the workday she felt like a dead astronaut floating in space.

On the way home Sarah vomited in the train-station bathroom like she always did.

She vomited in the bathroom like taking mail out of a mailbox.

She tickled her half-brother and was really silly that night after drinking 1 blue moon because she didn't have any food in her stomach.

Nipple Mystery

H met a woman at the bar. H liked the woman at the bar so he missed the last train for her. They drank mojitos. The woman at the bar talked about the interconnectedness between the universe and all of the objects within it etc.

The woman at the bar invited H back to her apartment. The apartment was very chillin. The woman had a terrarium of Macaqs in the middle of her apartment. H said "your monkeys are very pretty" and the woman said thank you.

H and the woman made out.

Then, they took off their clothes. It was when they disrobed that H noticed something very weird.

"Where in the wide world of sports are your nipples?" H said. The woman indeed had 2 breasts, but 0 nipples. This woman was a freak of nature.

"Fuck," said H. "Are you a man?"

The woman laughed a high, feminine laugh. "Wait," she said, "you mean you didn't know what all happened regarding the nipples?"

"?"

She laughed again in the same unambiguously feminine way. "Kiss my grits...You must not have seen a pair of breasts for two whole years! That's when all our nipples vanished."

H blanched. "What do you mean 'Our?'"

"Why, I mean mine and every woman on planet earth's nipples," said the woman in a matter-of-fact tone.

H sat on the bed and ate his immense disbelief. It took him a few minutes. It had been six years since his last brush with coitus.

"Well...is this gonna be a problem?" asked the woman.

"No," H lied.

Without nipples, the woman's breasts had an "unconsummated" feel to them. He couldn't put his finger on why this was. He couldn't put his finger or his mouth on a nipple either. Putting his mouth where the nipple should have been left a shiny wet dome and didn't seem to turn her on.

INTERMISSION

After they had done a merry dance of sex H asked the woman "So what was it like adjusting to not having nipples?"

"Well, I didn't really care, to be honest," said the woman. "I mean, nipples don't do a whole lot. In the two years since they went away I've felt more and more that in the end all I lost were two tiny appendixes growing on my boobs."

H did not say, but he disagreed with the woman. Nipples held more seats in congress than appendixes, for damn sure. They were the ears and eyes of the Mammary gland. H curled up under the covers.

He regarded his companion, who was preparing to enter sleep-mode. She had Helen Keller nipples.

They went to sleep, woke up, and H left the woman's apartment with a mission on his mind.

The mission was to make sure that this nipple-business was not simply some freak-woman's special way of fucking with guys' heads.

In order to make his mission a mission accomplished he would (squirm) have to ask girls uncomfortable questions. H sighed. He needed to ask three random women. A small convenience sample of this size would decisively indicate whether or not the rest of earth's female population had lost their nipples too.

At the train station, H asked a girl awkwardly if her nipples had disappeared two years ago. It was so awkward, the way he asked her. Her response was awkward. And what's more, it was also a "yes." In his head, H apologized to the woman from the bar for thinking of her as a freak-

woman. For better or for worse, It
seemed now that she was a normal
woman with normal pockets of empty
space on her breasts instead of
nipples. H felt like a jerk. The girl who
had responded awkwardly gave H
sidelong glances until the train arrived.

When H went home he asked his Mom
if her nipples had disappeared
too. She said no. H whooped and
hollered with joy.   He had discovered
a glitch in the nipple-matrix. Why of
all people was his mother immune to
the effects of the nipple-exodus? He
had found a piece to the puzzle...a
piece that suggested this nipple-puzzle
was far larger than he had
imagined. Could there be a connection
between his mother still having nipples
and his being so elegantly out of the
nipple-loop? H was one step closer to
unraveling the mysteries that had been
plaguing him since the previous
night. Or so he thought.

"I'm just kidding! I don't have any nipples either," said H's Mom. "April Fools!"

H went to Subway before work. The Subway was empty, except for three female Subway employees. H asked all of them at the same time,if they had nipples. They looked at him weird.

The flight of the nipples was old news to them. To the female Subway employees, it was as though H was campaigning for a deceased former President. His voice made them bored. "Yep," said one of the girls. "Those nipples have been watching over us from heaven for the last two years. How'd you not hear about it? You must not have many female friends."

This stung. H walked out of Subway without a sandwich thinking negative thoughts about himself. He wished he had more female friends besides his

Mom.

He decided not to ask the girls at work nipple-questions.

He looked up "disappearing nipples" on Google and found an article entitled "They're Gone!"

H felt certain that something was awry. How had he not been aware of the nipples' disappearance? Why had no one told him before? How had he been in the dark for the last two years?

Three words echoed in H's brain: no female friends.

H rolled up into a ball and commenced to rock back and forth on his bed, emitting a high pitched whine from his throat. "This will reduce my anxiety about not having any female friends," thought H.

His Mom should have told him. She'd probably just forgotten. H worked when she was home; she worked when he was home.

To H, this was no excuse though. At 25, he could no longer rely on his mother to be his personal Geraldo Rivera. In the end, the blame rested on H's underdeveloped social-skills. H was taking a long, hard look at himself in the mirror. His self-esteem depended on his becoming more socially-involved and interested in his environment. News was key. If he knew what was going on in the news, he could use the information to start-up a conversation with another human.

Funny, the extent to which nipples motivated this man!

While looking at his Yahoo News feed, H caught a glimpse of his own nipples in the laptop screen. They were no good. A nipple was only good when attached to a breast. He wondered how he'd feel if all the breasts in the world disappeared. If all the breasts disappeared, one perk would be that no one would have to tell him because all of the women in the world would have flat chests. But really, even though the breasts were not perfect without nipples, H conceded that if he had a choice between the two, he would most definitely choose breasts.

So he let the whole nipple-thing go.

Pizza Restaurant Surprise

One day I was sitting in a pizza restaurant reading the *Psychopathia Sexualis* and eating a giant caesar salad. I was having a good time. Normally, I disliked being alive, but I was eating then and eating has always been an erotic experience for me. But my nice erotic time morphed into an un-nice erotic time when the chicken walked in. I am terribly frightened of chickens.

I pretended to go to the bathroom. As I walked down the hall, I could feel the chicken's orange eyes watching me suspiciously. I stood by the doors marked "M" and "F" and got out my phone, opening up the "Words-With-Friends" app. I played the word "fa" in a game I was losing. I assume "fa" means a long long way to run. I have "The Sound of Music" to thank for teaching me that word. Thank you, Sound of Music.

A woman came out of the restroom marked "F." She gave me a slightly perturbed look and walked briskly down the hall. However, when she got to the end of the hall, she turned all the way around and came back towards me.

"Are you hiding from that chicken?" she asked in a voice that sounded like my Mom's voice.

I nodded.

"Well, well, well," she said, a cherry blossom of contempt growing on her face, "I didn't think they allowed those beasts in public anymore."

"It's okay, I'm just going to wait until it goes away," I said, staring at my sneakers.

"No you're not!" she said sharply, "that thing is going to scat, if my name isn't Sestina Ararat" and Sestina marched down the hall towards the main dining area. I followed timidly, clutching my iPhone like a small chode-dagger.

"Hey punk," said Sestina to the chicken, "why don't you get the bleep out of here before I beat you down like Buffy the White Girl Slayer!"

"Bitch wut?" said the chicken, and he stood up, brandishing a laser-cutlass. The heat was on.

Sestina took a tiny pistol out of her purse and cartwheeled towards her adversary, and, as if the whole maneuver were a button-combo on Mortal Kombat, she plugged the chicken in its birdskull before he could tender a single slash. Droplets of chicken-blood fell on the chicken's half-eaten pizza.

The patrons looked aghast, as if someone had beheaded a goblin king or shot fire out of their hands. Whoever she was, the handfire of this mysterious woman had destroyed the head of the horrible animal whose presence had menaced me to such an extreme degree.

Unfazed, Sestinna got out her Android phone, speaking into it like a walkie-talkie. I heard her say "come dispose of it before the overworlders catch wind..."

When she'd finished she turned to me and said "wanna go somewhere where there aren't any chickens?"
"Hell yes!" I said
"Well, take hold of my hand and close your eyes." and I did.

When I opened my eyes I found myself

in a palace powdery and white. It looked like it was made of snow, but I didn't feel cold.

"Like it?" said Sestina, taking off her clothes, "it's all cocaine!"

"Jeez louise!" I exclaimed.

"grilled cheese" said Sestina.

Seventeen

I'm so fucking happy. Wanna know why? I'll tell you why, but I've gotta tell you a story first...

 I was waiting in line at a sandwich shop when an an enormous chicken walked in. I hastily pretended to go down the hall to the bathroom - I am very frightened of large chickens.

Standing by the bathroom door I busied myself with the Words-With-Friends game on my iPhone. I made the word "et," which means "and" in french. A beautiful girl came out of the the ladies restroom across the hall. She was wearing a ginormous purple sweater. When she saw me she stopped and flashed me a big friendly smile.

"Hello!" she said, "you look pretty! Would you like to go on a date with me?"

"I would," I said, "but there's this big chicken in line and I'm afraid of big chickens."

"Oh you poor thing! I'm sorry you're having to go through this. Here - I'll stand with you so you won't get bored."

I smiled, "That would be very sweet of you."

"No problem! You're cute and I don't want you to be scared. Here, I'll even hold your hand."

I blushed and said "awww."

She smiled her big friendly smile again "my name's seventeen, what's yours?"

So Seventeen and I got to talking. Her dad named her seventeen because it was his favorite sounding number in the number alphabet. She said she couldn't wait for the chicken to go away so she could go for a walk with me on this sunny day and then take me back to her apartment and fuck the shit out of me like a howler monkey on MDMA. She stroked my hair excitedly as she told me this.

When the chicken sat down to eat his sandwich, we went into the men's restroom together so he couldn't see us.

"would you like to have sex in the bathroom right now," asked Seventeen. Seventeen was extremely horny.

"No, I want to wait til later. Besides, what with the chicken and all, I think I'm too nervous to sustain an erection."

"That's totally okay," said Seventeen, nodding understandingly.

We went into one of the stalls to sit down. Both of us had tiny enough butts that we could sit on one seat together. We talked about music and how music was a drug that got you through the day. She put her head on my shoulder and watched me play Words-With-Friends. When I got 39 points on a triple word score she said "way to go!"

But just then, the chicken walked in.

"Oh no," I said in a high pitched voice. "Don't worry," said Seventeen, "I'll protect you."

The chicken opened the door to our

stall and came in, closing it behind him. Seventeen jumped up to face the chicken.

"If you want this boy, you'll have to kill me," said Seventeen.

The chicken regarded her with his malevolent orange eyes for a moment. Then, he pounced. Seventeen pulled a large ray gun out from underneath her purple sweater and fired at the avian freak-of-nature, vaporizing his head. It was my turn to say "way to go!"

We ordered sandwiches with relaxed expressions on our faces and took them to go, so we could get away before someone found the chicken's headless body and called the police. We took a lover's walk in the park, debating over how many babies we wanted to have. Seventeen said she wanted 100 babies, but I wanted more like 50. She said if we had 100 we could take over a small town. Once we had the town, we could make it the best small town in America. We would teach our children and the children of the town-we'd-take-over's townsfolk how to manufacture Seventeen's vapo-ray.

"Then, we'll take over the whitehouse and kill president whatever-his-name-is."

Seventeen's words swirled around my brain like a parade of tinkerbells. All of the things she was saying rang true. What better way to live? Making everybody else just like us. Seventeen and I were different sorts of people from the mainstream and we had chosen to be different because we had realized that it was better to be that way. I wanted to make Seventeen's dream come true - but first, we had to make a whole lot of babies.

...And that's why I'm so happy! I'm

having condomless sex on a regular basis with a wonderful, inspiring woman who protected me from a chicken, and 50 years from now I am going to be military governor of America and kill all of the chickens in the world.

Pterodactyl

I made no noise and did nothing. The
left and right hemispheres of my
brainground together. Sparks flew.

Birds flew outside. They made noise,
said hello to one another. They built
nests also.

I thought about buying tape,
optimistically. Then I thought about
dying.

I remembered a guy in the psych ward
who said he spent one whole day with
a blanket over his head.
 "I've done that before!" said the
brain-damaged schizoaffective sitting

next to me. The presiding therapist looked down at her notes with an uncomfortable expression on her face.

I put the blanket over my head and told myself I was okay. Then I said "I hate myself and turned into a pterodactyl. I flew out the window, de-atomizing the glass as I went.
I ate one of the birds outside. It squeaked as I crunched down on its body.

I took three victory laps around my apartment complex, shrieking imperiously.
A Christian youth group walking by looked up and saw me and felt excited because they were seeing a pterodactyl and then felt sad because the existence of pterodactyls contradicted the Bible.

The Bible was a unique book written many centuries ago. It was the only book in the world that decreased cognitive function in its readers.

I flew back into my room. I re-atomized the window. Then I ate a carrot and read the first 20 books of the Bible, destroying 1/16 of my brain. The 1/16th of my brain disappearing felt like a tiny underwater mine detonating.

"Oh no!" I said, "part of my brain just exploded! Oh well, maybe I'll find more things funny now."

To test my hypothesis I popped my ex girlfriend's roommate's copy of Glee Season 1 into the DVD player. I watched the first episode and did not understand any of the words. Perhaps the Bible had destroyed the part of my brain that processed language. This made me sad so I pressed my forehead against the cold, dimpled wall and meditated. Maybe I needed to go back to the hospital. Part of me wished I could stay in hospital for the rest of my life.

I turned into a pterodactyl again and ate my TV. Then I de-atomized the universe flying out into the nothingness. When tired, I slept, falling through the space once occupied by the earth, galaxies, and asteroids, and space.

The color of the space once occupied by the universe was yellow.

This all went on for a long time, my flapping and falling through the yellow. However, as was always the case, THE EVIL THING saw what was going on and pressed the button and I dropped out of the yellow and onto my bed, in human form.

I felt shitty. I tried to please myself by imagining a world in which all of the trees were replaced by helicopters, the wind gently nudging the propellers on a perfectly temperate autumn day.

All I have ever wanted in my life was for the rules that govern reality to be different. One day, in a deathmatch with THE EVIL THING this will happen. I have faith.

A Rat Sneaked Into The Refrigerator

Bobby was sitting at his kitchen table playing a game on his phone when three dark shapes came to the door.

Bobby saw them through the blinds but he couldn't make out their features.

One of the figures knocked, and Bobby cautiously went and answered the door.

When he opened the door he let out a cry of surprise, for the three dark shapes on the threshold of his house were still as indistinct as he had seen them through the blinds. Silhouettes with bits and pieces of colorful fuzz.

"Who are you?" said Bobby

"We're the people you didn't notice who noticed you today," said the first indistinct figure.

"We had lots of thoughts about you and wondered where you were going, but you didn't even look at us or think about us."

"We looked at you and thought that you had it all together, and felt jealousy towards you, but also this difficult feeling to describe...like you weren't attractive or anything, but you were likeable."

"I watched you listen to your iPod for almost an hour, commuting from work"

"So that's why we're here."

"I'm sorry, I'm afraid I don't know what to say," said Bobby "What do you want from me?"

"All we want is for you to look really hard at us," said the third figure, "really take the time to study us and think about us a little bit."

"Um, okay." said Bobby, "well I guess you'd better come in."

Bobby took a seat at his kitchen table, and the three dark figures sat down as well. And for a while Bobby just stared.

He didn't know why he should oblige these three apparitions, but he felt he should. He looked really hard at them. No one spoke. There was a lot of Bobby staring at the three indistinct figures.

After about half-an-hour, the shadowy

figures started coming into focus. One was a white man in a business suit that looked very well to do. There was a black woman, about Bobby's age, who had gauges in her ear and was wearing a band t-shirt. The last was a young hispanic man with shiny gelled hair and a backpack - probably a student.

"Okay," said Bobby, now that I can see you, what should we do?"

"You have to become facebook friends with us," said the young black woman.

Bobby considered this.

"hmm well I guess I can manage that."

"Excellent," said the white man in the suit

"Good to meet you man, you seem like a chill person," said the Hispanic student.

"We'll exchange contact info later," said the young black woman.

And then they all said goodbye and Bobby closed the door.

Bobby sat down at the kitchen table again and resumed the game he had been playing earlier. After about 15 minutes he got hungry and went to the fridge.

He opened the fridge door and saw a rat.

The rat was holding a sign that said, "there's too many people in the world."

Jimmy and His Motorcycle

When church finished and the preacher sat down in his chair, I got up from my pew at the back and cut out. I didn't feel like going home yet so I stood against John X. Rivers's statue for awhile. The trees lining the town square have always been really interesting to me. They snake up, almost higher than the church, par with the top of the Christdome, nearly all reticulated trunk, with a tiny green canopy the size of Joseph Spencer's Jacuzzi. That Jacuzzi's about man-sized. A man can utterly submerge himself there, just him by himself. I allow myself to ask Joseph if I can lie there about once (or sometimes twice) every two months. I just lie there with my ears under but my face not and listen to the slow sounds of the water gurgling in and out. The congregation filed out slowly, the various men and wives. I saw Padre Nikolai. He's a friend of Preacher Padre Mac. Was a good preacher in his day. He was actually my preacher for awhile. I'd go to the church just to hear his sermon. My girlfriend says he's pretty nice. When I was a kid he said such good things, but he stopped when I was I guess 14 and started his Ministry On Four Legs which everybody in Centerville calls Pet Church. He has a fantastic tan and still looks as young as he looked back then. He has this real tranquil atmosphere around him. He was with his new wife. She's real pretty and skinny with blonde hair. Padre Nikolai recognized me and waved and I waved back and smiled. Their car came to pick them up obediently. They have a great car. I see it a lot. Green with lots of ridges and sophisticated looking highbeams.

When they left, I got bored and decided I'd saddle up my motorcycle, and I coasted around Church square for about half an hour, listening to the Carter Family on the boombox taped to the backseat, listening to them sing Foggy Mountain Top. I've had the motorcycle since I was a teenager. It's got a lot of power. Sometimes, when it's run out of gas, it keeps going through the juice in its own metal. The square here, with the church at its center, is lined with stores. There are only two ways to get inside the square: two skinny one way streets at latitudes directly north and south of the church. There's a grocery store, with oranges and limes in cardboard boxes out front and a little man on a motorized chair, who despite his soft gummy 1 toothed face and tiny red head, has lived a beautiful long life and husbanded a plethora of wives, who all gave him something beautiful. Like a tiny red trophy, he waves as I pass, and every time I notice, but don't

acknowledge him. I should, I know.
He is an elder and I must respect him.
I mean, he's so holy he doesn't even
go to church. He just has so much
grace. Everybody says so. But I just
feel so nervous and remote every time
I make that left turn on the Northeast
corner. I feel nervous around him and
a lot of other people. Padre Nik is one.
But I have a connection with him
through my courtship of his daughter
so I've gotten more okay around him
lately. I don't acknowledge him, even
though, through my sunglasses, I am
staring, with my eyes open wide.   I
wear very dark sunglasses. Joseph
Spencer said one time that the lenses
are so dark they could have been
made from material mined on the dark
side of the moon.

"The motherfucking dark side of the
moon," he said with his beer and his
ugly beard.

"You should shave your beard," I said,

"don't mock my ways of getting girls
cuz you're too ugly to get girls."

"Fuck you," he said and shook his head
and his ugly beard.

He knows I'm joking. This is just the
way we're friends with each other. I
wouldn't ever say a bad thing about
Joseph Spencer. He is a fine man.
Though I suppose I do say bad things
about him sometimes to my other
friends. The way you just have to
sometimes, when you're living with
someone.

I'm actually only half sure he knows
I'm joking. Maybe it does hurt him
and he just doesn't say. It says in the
bible that there are the three outer
kingdoms: the world, hell, and heaven
and that also, in addition, there are the
four subkingdoms: Inner Heart, Outer
heart, Outer brain and Inner Brain.
God told the disciples that the outer
brain and outer heart are apparent,

but that the inner brain and inner heart are hidden, and that we must, through faith, give credence to the possible hidden thoughts and feelings and be respectful and that by making our inner hearts and inner brains respectful, our outer organs are better able to be respectful and viser verser. It is only within the bonds of family, business partnership, and marriage that the Inner Heart and Inner Brain can be completely revealed to another human being. Joseph Spencer has surprised me in the past with revelations of his inner organs. If he knows anything about my disrespect or suspects anything in my manner…he is a fine man. He would be my best man if I got married, but I don't think I'll be getting married any time soon. Marriage, and the owning of property, and keeping women happy. Gee Whizz. I don't know if I'll ever get married.

I'm 25. Most all of the boys in my high school class got married when they were 24. People who don't get married just leave town and get into trouble and go to jail, so I guess I'll probably go to jail.

I've been in trouble before when I was a teenager. I punched a man at Long Selby's who hadn't done anything but say something about my Dad and it was bad. They took away my motorcycle and locked me up and gave me medicine for my temper and that's when Ruby went away and started dating Cody Jones, that goddang tight end. But I got my motorcycle back. It wouldn't let no one else ride it and anyhow, I didn't try to run over the fucker. So I'm glad for that. Me and my motorcycle have been through a lot.

"Hey, where ya going?" Joseph said as I open up the garage door

"I'm going to pick up my girl,"

"Which girl?"

"Heather."

"Yeah?"

"Yeah."

"Okay. Well if y'all smoke, do it in the garage."

"Yeah man," I turn the key and the motorcycle gets really happy cuz it's gonna get to go out on the road.

"Okay. Take it easy," says Joseph Spencer waving his prop, the beer. It's a terrific evening. There's an aurora right at where the still-light part meets the shutter of darkness. I keep my sunglasses on.

Most motorcycles are good at smoking weed. They don't cough and never make any noises of disgust when you or your friends cough. Up until recently, I'd never had a problem with it but it just started coughing a ton and it's really embarrassing when I try to get high with my girlfriends. I talked to Joseph Spencer about it and he said it was probably getting old, but I know that isn't right. Motorcycles live for thirty years and usually more. It is said that old Preacher Padre John X. Rivers who founded Centerville rode his for a hundred and seven years. I have girlfriends in Northville, girlfriends in Southville, girlfriends in Westville, and girlfriends in Eastville. I take them out in the order I mentioned them in, one girlfriend a night. We usually go get high, and then go get hamburgers. But you see, just lately, my motorcycle's been coughing and making noises of disgust when other people cough. We all get in a circle in my friend Joseph Spencer's garage and pass around the pipe: the girl I'm dating gets the first hit, I get the second, and my motorcycle gets the third, as motorcycles ought to, considering they do not have the holy spirit inside of their cold metal bodies. The motorcycle coughed and it also laughed at my girlfriend Heather when she let out a cough with her little pink lungs. Her beautiful little pink lungs, my motorcycle laughed at them, and she cried and her little pink lungs palpitated cutely as she did. I was so irate! I almost broke god's 2nd property commandment: Thou shalt not damage Father God's machines and human furnishments. After the motorcycle coughed and laughed, the girl and I went to Long Selby's to get hamburgers. It's called Long Selby's because when you go inside, there aren't any tables and chairs, only a long counter that stretches for one hundred feet with barstools dotted down its spine at neat and ordered intervals. When you lean back, your head touches the window. We arrived at the restaurant on foot and we knocked on the door and waited while the restaurant attendant came to let us in. We sat down and got to watch our hamburgers get made on their hamburger assembly line. There was some Carribean music playing on the jukeboxes. Not stupid bob marley. REAL Carribean music, with clicks and tin splashes and yeah yeah yeah. I bought Heather an enormous hamburger, but I wasn't hungry. My motorcycle, now seemingly bereft of its tokers-etiquette, had totally killed my smoke hunger. I developed a plan in my head, as the Carribean music clicked and splashed tinnily. The plan developed was long and intricate, as long as Long Selby's but a bit more intricate than Long Selby's was. If my plan was a restaurant, it would be a long version of Macaroni Grill. I ordered my girlfriend another hamburger as I pondered and stared out across the parking lot, my leather-jacketed back leaned up against the bar, my thumbz in my jean-pockets, my boots on the window. This was a plan that would take me further than any coughing motorcycle.

"Hey," I said

"Yeah," said heather.

"You've performed exorcisms, right?" I said, turning my stool slowly around to face her.

"Nooooo, that's not what I said," she said, "I said 'I watched ma daddy do exorcisms on Dog's at petchurch."

"Oh, that's right. I forgot" I said, looking down the long countertop.

"You need to listen more. In relationships you have to listen. That's what you're supposed to do. Listen. Listen to your girlfriends. Otherwise-" she picked up her fork and turned towards me a quarter-turn. "Otherwise, you won't be able to control us...and you know what happens then..."

She was fooling. I could tell. I knew she was just real heated up and trying to act tough cuz she knew I was feeling disheartened and she wanted to fire me up. I have been disheartened for a long time. When I was a kid I wasn't so disheartened. Only a little bit disheartened. But as my body grew longer and I started growing a beard and feeling the Master's Pleasure my heart seemed to travel further and further away from my head and now it is so far away I can't even see it for the shadows and junctions of passageways.

"Say, you know that that was what I meant, baby," I said. "Your daddy does do exorcisms."

"No duh, you woulda known if you had listened," she rolled her eyes. I ignored her.

"Do you think I could get your Daddy to perform an exorcism on my set-of-wheels?"

"I don't know," she said, taking a bite of her hamburger and chewing pensively. "He usually only does exorcisms on dogs and cats and sometimes bunnies."

"Okay, well we'll see. I'll call him on the telephone."

"When are you gonna call him on the telephone? He's very busy."

I thought a moment and then said "when the sun rises, when the first bluebird's wing peeks across the threshold of its cave, when the alarm clock in Joseph Spencer's garage rings, when the old retarded lady across the street from your house wakes up screaming... that's when I'll call."

"Do you really have to, Jimmy?"

"Yeah, I do. Baby, I can't have my motorcycle laughing when you cough on hits. It's okay for you to cough, darlin'. For you it just means that you have healthy lungs, reacting innocently to the fiery cannabis fumes – for a motorcycle, it means it's a foul-spirited motorcycle – and what's more, a pussy motorcycle with an un christlike attitude. And I can't have that. I can't have no motorcycle who's gonna make disrespectful noises when you cough. I can't have that, baby. And if that motorcycle's gonna do that with you, there's no telling what it'll do when my other girlfriends come over."

"Yeah, I guess," she said. "But baby," and here she put her hand on my cheek, "be careful. Exorcism's a risky business. You could get your nose plowed through and talk like a duck for the rest of your life."

"Quack, quack," I said in a duck voice. She giggled like a jar of nuts, and the night went on, and the authentic Carribean music played, and I drove her home on my motorcycle, and I gave her a peck on the cheek on the front steps of her large becolumned mansion, and then I went over to Joseph Spencer's place, and he asked me how it went and I said "It was good. I don't know if I can sleep tonight. I have a phone call in the morning" and then he gave me some speed, and he took some too and we stayed up all night talking about how our families made us the way they did and how we're learning to get over it. Joseph Spencer is a chunky white-pink man who dresses like a hobo and has an unattractive looking Mohawk. A lot of the time he wears a long trench-coat and grins stupidly. He has a degree in creative writing and he is using it to- and all of a sudden the alarm went off and like a pavlovian dog, I flicked open my sprint-phone and dialed 972-972-9722. As fast as a thirteen year old girl who'd just seen her first boyfriend's name on the caller ID, Padre Nikolai picked up.

"To whom am I talking at?" he said shrilly.

"This is Jimmy. I'm one of Heather's boyfriends," I said. I had a lot of respect for Padre Nik. Sometimes I had dreams that he was my father in a very abstract way. In one dream, he is a giant vampire bat who is carrying me in a basket across a green sea, towards a blue mountain. I never had a daddy of my own and sometimes I look for a daddy in the faces of my friends' daddys.

"Ah yes," said Mr. Vampire Bat.

"You're the one who likes listening to the Carter Family."

"Uh huh, that's exactly right," I said, "one of my favorite things to do on Sunday afternoons after church is duct-tape my friend Joseph Spencer's boom-box to the back seat of my motorcycle and drive around and around church square listening to the Carter Family and wearing black sunglasses...and sometimes I feel so empty and hollow when I do this because I don't have a daddy to watch me ride my motorcycle and see me as a mature and independent man...and I want a daddy so bad, goddamnit, but I'm never going to have a daddy because he died when my mother killed him when I was in the bath, naked and young with blonde hair. She was a very large woman and he was a very small man. She pressed his forehead onto the cold metal table in the garage after she'd made him take his shirt off and he flailed his arms and cried like a bitch stuck in a bear-trap, and my mother said 'I don't want you raisin' my kid. You're not a good dad. I'm gonna cut off your fingers and then stab you in the back of the head.' And my Dad shrieked and I sat in the bath with frog fingers and lukewarm water, crying. And my father bless his soul screamed very loudly and woke up our neighbors who knew about the way my mother abused my father and they called 911, but the police came too late to save my dad. He was 5'3" and she was 6'7" and she didn't give him a chance. She was like a wild animal when she didn't take her pills or meditate. When the police came they had to shoot her, because she would've killed them if they didn't. My mother was away all the time when I was a little kid, shopping her Yuri Manga at various anime conventions across the country, and my Dad took care of me at home and read me Swiss Family Robinson before I went to sleep. And then he was gone, my sweet Daddy was gone..."

"I'm sorry," said Mr. Vampire Bat "I'm sorry you had to go through that, son."

"I...I don't know," I said sheepishly. "I think I went a little off topic...I'm sorry."

"It's alright, son...I know that stuff like this happens sometimes...like, you're just going along, doing the stuff you normally do and then BOOM you just gotta let it all out. And Jimmy, listen: this is a safe place, I am a safe place to let things out. These days, I am mainly concerned with the spiritual lives of the animals who come to my pet-church, but..."

And on the other line there was a pause long enough for a wink

"...people are animals too, and I can be your shepherd, Jimmy. Would you like that? Would you like me to be your shepherd in these dark times, Jimmy?"

"Yes, Padre Nikolai. I'd like that a lot."

"Well, why don't you come over for dinner tonight?"

"That's really swell of you, Padre Nikolai, but I had already planned for my girlfriend Charlene and I to go out to Long Selby's for hamburgers-"

"Up bup bup!" said Padre Nikolai, "from what my daughter tells me, you go to Long Selby's an awful lot."

"But I like Long Selby's, Padre Nikolai."

I was angry at Padre Nikolai for suggesting such a thing as not going to Long Selby's. My brow clenched and my hands trembled with barely suppressed rage. Who did he think he was, messing up my schedule?
"But you've also got to broaden your horizons, kid," Padre Nikolai said. His tone of voice was that of a light wind muzzing a child's hair. "I think the fact that you go to a long restaurant signifies that you put a lot of distance

between yourself and everything...including yourself, if that makes sense. You should try moving closer to new ideas, rather than distancing yourself from them with familiar things like Long Selby's. You should try moving closer to Jesus. That restaurant is such a long restaurant. Why do you think you go to such a long restaurant?"

"I don't know, Padre Nikolai," I said, "but I have an inkling that it's because I'm afraid of going to farther away, smaller restaurants where everything's close together on the inside. I have a hard time with things being close to me, except my motorcycle. I keep my motorcycle close. It's almost like a twin, but like a twin who's also the mother I never had. But nevertheless, when I go to Long Selby's with my girlfriends I keep my motorcycle in my friend Joseph Spencer's garage."

"Just out of curiosity," said Padre Nikolai, "where do your other girlfriends live? Are they also Eastville Middle School girls like my sweet little booboboo?"

I told him where my other girlfriends lived.

"Wow! You drive to all those different locations?   Don't you live in Centerville?

"Yeah. Why?"

"Well all that mileage must be taxing on your motorcycle."

"I always have money for gas," I said, flexing my black gloved hand as if testing it's squeeze-power. "My girlfriends always give me gas money, as long as I give them lots of kisses."

"You don't want to give your girlfriends too many kisses," he said, "if you give

225

them too many kisses, they start to get cocky and become excited too easily, flapping their arms and making weird whistling noises for no reason. No you don't want that – whereabouts you want your girls' dispositions to be is right between a shiny silver Caribbean fish and a cat. So, don't give them too many kisses. But I don't have to tell you that. I trust your judgement"

"Thank you, Padre Nikolai," I said, a large smile broadening on my face. "Even so, your advice is good advice and I will treasure it like my motorcycle, like my friendship with my friend Joseph Spencer who allows me to crash at his place when I don't have my own place to live, even when I sometimes say and do things that annoy him, and don't listen to him, and make fun of him when I talk to my girlfriends or my other male friends." There were a lot of strange, violent emotions running up and down my skin like crawling streams of cold sap. Every moment I shivered. I'd left my context. I was too choked up to say anything to Padre Nik. I was a traveler, who had stepped off his boat and into the sea only to find he could walk across it.

"I...I was going to ask you if you could do an exorcism when I called you on the telephone."

"Yes," he said, "my daughter told me. She said you were gonna give me a call when the lady across the street started screaming, because apparently, she starts screaming at the exact same time the alarm clock in your friend's basement goes off...and also...when a bird comes out of its cave?"

"Yeah. Yeah, man."

At this point, Joseph Spencer ambled into the garage wearing boxers and a

T-shirt that said "Follow the Stream." Assuming I was in the middle of an important phone call, he gave me a sleepy nod and trudged over to where his motorcycle stood. He got out his toolbox and tended to his bike, prodding and brushing with the stainless steel instruments as if it were a garden or a baby – such grace and tenderness he employed! He tightened nuts, pumped tires – phew! What a guy!

Down the road, down blocks, through blocks, over blocks, to the outskirts of town to that big, pine covered hump of hill, through the overgrowth, through the dead leaves, the beetles, over the rocks as our perspective climbs higher...in a crumbled lean-to of granite which creates a dark aperture, the cave, we come and we sit. There are crumbled down flat white rocks everywhere and trees, pine trees as well. And out of the cave the bluebird hops, from rock to rock. Two tweets.

Critical hyper swivels of the neck birds have. One hop and whoosh! Off it goes into the morning light. It flies over Long Selby's, and darts down onto the roof, just above Selby's long thumb giving the thumbs up. It twitters there. Looks around. Looks down. By the parking-space line. 2 in. away. Sees gum. A patch of black gum with a little white crumpled up piece of paper in it. Bluebird flies down, lands on the tarmac. Hops toward the gum, and more particularly, the piece of paper. Hop, hop, hop. The bird leaned down and picked up the piece of paper with its beak. It realigns its beak to hold it and then with a flutter skips back up into the sky. There is something written on the paper, but it doesn't matter because birds can't read. It continues its errands. Later that day, it flies over a mansion. A mansion with columns. Two figures are walking up the Mansion's steps.

Me and Charlene walked up the mansion steps. I was wearing a tuxedo and she was wearing a sparkling golden dress made out of gold diamonds that she'd bought for the occasion. She has the most beautiful brown hair I have ever seen and a small face with little eyes and a little nose and a little mouth with purple lips. She comes up to about my armpit.

"I'm ner-vusss," she said.

"It's okay sugar darlin'," I said, "Mr. Vampire Ba-I mean Padre Nik's a wonderful man. And also, my girlfriend Heather is a wonderful, beautiful young lady, and you're wonderful and beautiful too, so y'all should all get along."

We rang the doorbell. We stood on rose colored bricks while we were waiting for them to come to the door. The door was mahogany with a gold letterbox. I admired the columns. They were huge, like oak trees. My motorcycle was parked on the curb, whistling its lil' ol' waiting song. Sweet-woo, sweet-woo, whistled the motorcycle.

"Hi! Come on in!" said Padre Nikolai as Heather opened the door. Padre Nikolai's hand was on Heather's shoulder. Her eyes were bright and attractive. She smiled excitedly when she saw Charlene. They had on the same dress!

"You have impeccable taste!" she said to Charlene, emphasizing the word impeccable.

"Thank yooou," said Charlene both emphasizing the word "you" and protracting it.

"Ha! Come on in!" said Padre Nikolai again.

Padre Nikolai's house was a house of God indeed. There were animals everywhere. Cats, dogs, you name it! They had it all. The two Dominant Wives of Padre Nikolai greeted us as well. They'd been cookin' up a feast. Jorda wore a grass skirt and a black tank top. She was heavier than Kristy, who wore a bikini.

"Yeah, we've been cooking all day," said Kristy, moving her tanned leg to the side to let a big dog walk by.

"Hope ya'll like Macaroni!"

"And we hope ya'll like jerk-pork and beans" said Jorda in a loud voice, walking in from the kitchen. She was a very attractive chubby older woman. Long, carrot-red hair and bronze skin, with blue, bluebird eyes.

As Jorda and Kristy did the dishes, Padre Nikolai and I sprawled out on his fluffy, meaty armchairs which were in the living room. Heather and Charlene had decided to go swimming. We could hear the clatter of dishes through the opening in the French doors which led to the kitchen. There was a chandelier with giant rubies. Rubies as big as mine and Padre Nikolai's heads. We unbuttoned our pants to let our guts hang out. My underwear was tight as well, so I pulled it up to give my guts a little more room.

"Ah!" said Padre Nikolai.

"Mhm," I said, "your wives cooked so much macaroni and cheese, I think I'm about to go nova! I tell you what..."

"What does 'go nova' mean?" asked Padre Nikolai, somewhat perplexed.

"Oh," I said, "It's just what scientists call a star blowing up in scientist-slang."

"uh-huh...hee hee...nova, that's good...heh, that's good..." He laughed quietly, closing his eyes.

"Thank you for inviting us," I said.

"Don't mention it." He was super-relaxed. I was relaxed too. I kept looking over at him, looking at his relaxation.

"So," I said, "I wanted to thank you again..." he looked up and smiled. "I want to thank you again, for being my shepherd." My eyes teared up. He put his hand on my shoulder and gripped it, looking me directly in the eye. His eyes were dark brown. I could see my reflection in them. "It's okay to cry, son," he said.

"Naw," I said, turning away. He didn't take his hand away from my shoulder. "I'm not gonna cry. There are lots of things to do. Gotta get a job. Start going to school. Gotta get an apartment. Gotta move out of Joseph Spencer's house." I wiped the tears away from my eyes. He kept his hand on my shoulder. Then he took it off.

"Here," he said, and he picked up a puppy that had been sleeping by the chair."Ya see this little dog?"

"Yeah," I said. "It's a cute dog."

"Yes. It's a cute dog. And you might not be able to fathom this, (the dog is so cute, I can hardly fathom it) but this dog, when I found it on the street 2 months ago, was talking to me with the voice of Satan. It was telling me that nobody loved me, that my parish for animals was stupid, that I'd never be able to save all the animals, that my wives didn't respect me, that my daughter was ugly – all these horrible things..."

The dog didn't look satanic at all. It was just a little puppy dog with a cute face. It had a cute wet nose right next to its cute lips and its cute teeth. Padre Nikolai rubbed its head while it breathed fast and happy.

"This dog was saying all this bad stuff that I just didn't want to listen to, couldn't listen to. I'm a member of the clergy. I don't want to hear this...this trash! I have a mission from God, God came to me in a dream and told me he wanted me to protect and save and be righteous and that's what I do." He spat out his gum. A tortoiseshell cat came over and ate it up.

"So, you know what I did?"

"Whatidja do?"

"I grabbed it by its neck and walked two blocks from the bus stop back to the pet church, and I went inside and I sprayed him with Demon-Gas and I turned on the sound system, turned on the frequencies and I sat there and held it on the metal table I have in there until the voice stopped shouting. I held it there for two whole hours while he struggled and scratched my hands. Kristy called me on the telephone because I was late for dinner and I didn't pick up, so her and the wives just waited and they got upset. But when I finished," he looked up at the chandelier, "it was all worth it. And I have this beautiful animal. This beautiful animal...and he so swee-eet...there's no satan in you at all," he talked to the dog. "There's no satan in you at all, you're just one of Jesus' puppies ... hey...hey...you're wunna Jesus' puppies!" He let it back on the ground and the puppy dog scampered across the floor to the kitchen to go sniff the women.

"We should go outside," he said, getting up and buttoning up and zipping up his pants. "Go see what my daughter and your other girlfriend are doing."

I stood up too and began to follow him before turning around to address you, the reader:

"Was it fate? I've wanted to be friends with this guy ever since I met him when I picked Heather up from her house for the first time. I knew he was the missing piece of the puzzle, but I was shy. I thought that because he was an older man and that I was only 25, that we couldn't be friends. But look at us now! We're like Batman and Robin. I found out he really likes me too. Plus..." I turned back to see if Padre Nikolai was listening. He wasn't. He was just standing there inanimately in the doorway. Nevertheless, to the reader, I furtively whisper: "I'm thinking about marrying his daughter and Charlene in a couple months." I look back again. Only for effect. "I'm gonna wait awhile though. All this new happiness is gonna take a while to get used to." I pause in my soliloquy. Put on a thinking face. "Y'know, all this has got me thinking about this motorcycle of mine."

"Sweet woo," went the motorcycle outside.

"I would never have spilled my depression-beans to Padre Nikolai if it hadn't been for my motorcycle displaying signs of possession," I said thoughtfully. "Maybe the motorcycle did it deliberately! Maybe it sensed the tempest swirling around inside of my head and acted to save me...but that is an absurd notion..." I turn and make as if to follow Padre Nik. "Motorcycles can, of course, perform simple functions like eating and drinking and playing games," I said, "but they don't have souls...they can't have a consciousness...or can they?"
`

"Sweet woo," went the motorcycle.

As I went onto the deck outside, Padre Nikolai turned to me. "Shhhh!" he said.

The pool was only about 2 feet deep and the water looked beautiful, like it had been imported from the Bahamas. They sat there in the middle of the pool, naked, their hair glistening with jewel-like droplets. Charlene's nipples were darker than Heather's which were robin red. They hadn 't yet noticed our arrival and were studying each other curiously with both their eyes and their hands. Their gold-diamond dresses sat on the deck chair adjacent to me. The dresses twinkled in the sunlight like two golden rabbits huddled together. Their expressions were neither happy nor sad, just sensitive, or maybe sensatory, or maybe just sensing. It looked like the greatest feeling ever. An enormous wave of emotion swept over me.

"First thing tomorrow, I'm moving out of Joseph Spencer's garage!"

They both turned to look at me, and, though somewhat startled, they smiled.

Girls Laughing Genuinely

"Compositions are integrated within," said the woman's voice, "gen-up to electric-dog status. they pat you on the back, your ears prick up. They call you Hitler and then kick you around like homogenized milk." Then came the drum machine in 4/4 time.

Bobby lay on the floor next to the boombox, listening. He always liked the spoken-word introduction to The Fall song "C.R.E.E.P." He did not understand what the woman was saying. He liked it because it seemed negative and incomprehensible, just like him. Bobby stared into space and imagined girls laughing genuinely at a joke he had just thought of. Bobby was 15 years old and weighed 270 pounds and lived in America and was a type 4 on the Enneagram and masturbated every day. He was told by his mother that he possessed wisdom though he had no wisdom and never would. At this point in his life he bought lots of CDs and loved buying CDs more than anything else. This would be his obsession for two years. Then, for another four years he would be obsessed with working-out. Then for 15 years he would be obsessed with forming relationships with other people. Then, for the rest of his life, he would not be obsessed with anything and would try to do his job and stay on facebook when he was not doing his job.

"Compositions are integrated within," said the woman, "gen-up to electric-dog status. Your ears prick up. They pat you on the back and then kick you around like homogenized milk." Bobby stared at the orange streak of dusk-nearing sun falling on the Throbbing Gristle poster pinned to his wall. The song was on repeat. Bobby stared at the poster and imagined girls laughing genuinely.

Billy and Jorge and The Monotony of Life

I'm honest. I tell people what I think.
I don't care if they like it or not. I live
with my mom, but I pay rent and I
also pay insurance and car payments.
My parents are divorced. My dad's got
money. I work for him sometimes.
He pays me good money to give his
clients estimates, talking on the phone
and stuff. I've worked at the theatre
for two years. I make 9 dollars an
hour. I like whiskey. And Tequila. I
don't like vodka.

-Jorge

*

Billy nodded his head to appear as though he understood something. No one was watching him nod. The thing he thought he understood while nodding was a domestically concocted abstraction verbally caricaturized by the words "monotony of life."

Billy imagined himself being interviewed by Teri Gross and using the phrase "monotony of life" as he recollected the "period of transition," he saw his life in at that moment. He imagined his mannerisms in the interview as very similar to Rowan Atkinson's, or the mannerisms Rowan Atkinson had displayed in one interview he had seen.

Billy then felt courageous enough to articulate to himself the fact that the Rowan Atkinson interview he was using as a reference in his self-portrait of a Teri Gross subject was a mock interview he had seen in an episode of "Fry and Laurie."

In the mock interview, Rowan Atkinson had been reflecting on the life and career of Hugh Laurie as if he had recently died. Billy realized it was possible that Rowan Atkinson had been in character during the sketch.

Billy took comfort in acknowledging the truth that his persona in the imaginary interview derived from an actor participating in a farce, possibly employing the mannerisms of a character, and possibly not.

There was a source to the mannerisms he imagined, and however distorted his memory was, the fact that a trusted, coherent connection existed in his brain made him happy.

As Rowan Atkinson and Teri Gross darted around his skull, Billy went to the closet, grabbed a broom and dustpan, and began sweeping up the constellations of popcorn behind the concessions stand. With the auditorium-doors shut and the patrons under the big screen's spell, Billy was to watch the stand until Jorge finished eating his fried chicken. Then he could go on break.

It was "courageous" of Billy to articulate the truth to himself because he thought slowly and was afraid to take the time it took him to gather his honest thoughts and sentiments.

Billy would often haphazardly piece together replies with material that resembled a reasonable response, to avoid the embarrassment and anxiety of the inquirer losing interest and moving onto another train of thought.

- Billy

*

Billy's just really quiet. I don't know him too well. We went to a party together once and got drunk.

I do this thing where when I see him I say "Billy Bob Thornton" in a redneck hillbilly voice. Sometimes he laughs, sometimes he doesn't.

He's not the slowest at concession, but he's pretty slow.

He gets mad sometimes too.

I think he has really low self-confidence. I try to be nice to him.

-Jorge

*

Billy heard the familiar rattle of the scullery door and Jorge marched purposefully towards him.

"Billy! Billy Bob!" said Jorge.

"Hey," said Billy

"Oh, Billy Bob," said Jorge, poking Billy in the stomach, "Oh Billy Bob! I just want to squeeze your tits!"

Billy flinched, but laughed, and headed towards the scullery door, unbuttoning his work shirt to take off his magnetic nametag.

"Thanks Jorge," he said.

Jorge had messed with Billy when he first started working at the theatre, but in the past year they had settled into an amiable coexistence. In fact, a few months ago, Jorge had remarked one day "I miss Billy." Billy had laughed sarcastically when he had heard about this, but he'd been touched.

Billy punched in the keycode to the employees-only wing and walked up the steps to the break room. "The 6th Sense" was playing on the TV in concert with a loud discussion. 7 people were there, 3 on the sofa, 4 at the tables. He sat across from Howard, who had told him two weeks ago that Billy probably thought about things on a deeper level than most of the people they worked with.

Billy had wanted to become friends with Howard, but he was afraid of, in a weird way, overstaying his welcome in Howard's esteem.

Howard was really engaged in the conversation today

Billy didn't know why he had come to the break room. For him, walking into the break room was like walking into a room full of strobelights and sitting quietly as they flashed.

Billy listened, as always for the moment when the discussion shifted to something he knew about.

He always wondered how they all kept talking and making jokes. He thought it might be because they knew they were going to work minimum wage jobs until they died and were in such pain that they had to make jokes to maintain their sanity

Jorge wasn't like them, but he could still socialize. He didn't need to work minimum wage. His father could send him to college. Billy knew lots of people who were not condemned to working minimum wage who could still keep up a conversation.

What was it about Billy?

Billy asked himself that question at least 50 times a day.

Nothing that interested Billy was being said.

So when he got up and left, with the lassitude quietly watching lights flash for 10 minutes entails, he was taken aback when Sharon yelled "Oh no! Look what we did! We've scared away Billy!"

His coworkers always seemed to make a big deal about their conversations' subject matter being exceptionally crass or strange, when it really wasn't.

"No, no," said Billy, with a short nervous laugh, "I need to break someone."

Sharon laughed loudly at something someone else said and said another thing, and another thing, and then laughed at something someone else said, and then said another thing.
- Billy

*

My friend's in this one movie right now. I got him and his girl free tickets. I didn't give him free popcorn though, I can't do that anymore. Swiped my discount card. Man, y'know Andrea's kinda chubby, but she, man, if she lost like 10 pounds I'd bang her.
-Jorge

This book is dedicated to Tom Farris, whose laughter gave me the courage to push forward with this project.

About The Author

Harry McNabb is a solid route runner with soft hands. Think middle-to-late second round. He lives in Dallas, Texas and, also, a grape. .

Contact him at
mcnabbharry@gmail.com

CPSIA information can be obtained
at www.ICGtesting.com
Printed in the USA
FFHW010915240719
53817711-59536FF

9 780578 518930